Pylon by RM S

Table of Cont

Dedication:

For dad and the team of men he worked with.

Chapter 1. Waking-up

Harold reached over to silence the alarm, knocking it off the small table area built into the side of the fold-down bed. It was a practised move, the little metal clock with its stainless-steel case and two battered bells, received similar treatment six days a week. In fact, knocking the instrument off its perch was the only way to get it to silence the ringer. It was supposed to stop when you pushed down on the small handle that arched between the two bells. Unfortunately, even Harold's excellent mechanical skills had been unable to correct the fault. He had often tried fixing the errant instrument, usually spending an hour or two on a Saturday afternoon when there wasn't much else to do. Each time he would strip the mechanism down, taking care not to disturb the clock with its many brass cogs. Then he would meticulously rebuild the assembly in what should have been the correct manner.

Previous experience with similar timepieces had taught him about the consequences of disturbing the tightly wound steel springs. At the age of six, he had successfully disassembled his mother's alarm clock. He had been neat. First, placing a newspaper on the kitchen table, before beginning the delicate operation, each part laid out with almost military precision.

Putting that first clock back together should have been a case of working back through the ranks of cogs, springs, brass plates, and spacers. It would have, had he stopped at that point. Two coil springs had so-far eluded disassembly. They required tools which he didn't have. On each coil pack, a small shaft stuck out from the circular steel enclosure, which looked like a knitting needle thrust up through the top of an old top-hat.

The cover seemed to be separate from the shaft and the brim, secured by a crescent-shaped clip with small holes in the lugs at each end. Even then Harold knew there must be a special tool for dealing with clips like this one. Repeated and meticulous searches through his dad's toolbox, had failed to produce anything that might pull the ends of the clip apart.

Persistence and the deft handling of two small screwdrivers finally extracted one of the crescent-shaped clips from its groove in the main shaft. Gleefully he had removed the cover in anticipation of further cogs and gears to disassemble. Now as an adult, he winced at the remembered pain as the six-foot-long steel band whipped out slashing both his hands and face, enmeshing him in a web of inch wide steel band.

His mother had been horrified, swearing that he would never again be allowed to take anything apart. It had taken the doctor over an hour to remove the twisted band from around his arms and neck.

They had to use an old set of bolt cutters to cut through the spring steel. Had the cutters been new then each pump of the long handles would have snapped the metal ribbon cleanly. Unfortunately, they were worn and didn't quite make it through the extremely hard metal. Leaving just enough to stop the steel from coming apart. The doctor had to persistently wiggle the strip until the thin bit holding the steel broke. In a way, it was fortunate, that the doctor's grip on the ends of the spring prevented the jagged and razor sharp ends from inflicting more damage to his already sliced and diced body.

The net result was bandages and bed for two weeks. His mother had seen to it that all her husband's tools were relegated to the shed under lock and key. By her way of thinking it would be a long time before her only child would be allowed to risk his safety on the inside of another clock.

"Is it that time already?" Mavis asked, dreamily. Pulling herself closer to Harold. Her mind still on the previous night's lovemaking. Gently she inserted her left hand into his pyjama bottoms, lightly running her fingers along the sensitive crease between his leg and body. A move calculated to stimulate his desire for her. So far in the four years, they had been married it had never failed. Ensuring a warm and passionate rise most days of the week.

"Again?" Harold kidded, twisting himself around facing Mavis.

"You know if we keep this up I'll be old and knackered before I'm thirty." Returning her embrace by gently running the tips of his fingers over her right nipple, causing it to become large and firm. Her hand was having a similar effect lower down on his body.

"You are thirty." She chided, laughing. "And I've got some news for you."

"What news?" He asked dreamily, content to enjoy the delicate movement of her hand.

"I went to see the doctor yesterday." She paused, building the suspense, while gently increasing the stimulation.

"And?" Harold asked, lazily. Whatever her news was could wait.

"I'm four months pregnant." She informed him. Flipping him onto his back and sitting astride his muscular body. A move calculated to drive him wild with passion. This morning was no exception.

Ten minutes later they lay close still entwined in each other's arms, taking time to gather themselves for the coming day.

"So do you think it will be a girl or a boy then?" Harold asked gently kissing her still wet forehead. As usual, Mavis had retreated from the cold, under the heavy blankets, snuggling into his armpit, her head resting on his left shoulder.

"I don't know. What do you want it to be?" Harold paused, thinking for the first time in his life about what he wanted from a child.

"If it's a girl." His sentence trailed off for a few seconds.

"I don't know. As long as it's healthy and both of you are alright, I will be happy, He finally answered.

They continued to talk for five minutes or so, then the second alarm went off, a little tan leather travel clock that Mavis had bought just after they had come home from their honeymoon. Being more delicate than Harold's old clock Mavis always kept the second timepiece on the narrow shelf below the window at her side of the bed. Like most caravan dwellers objects migrated around the van during the day. A necessity born from the lack of usable space.

"Ok stud, time to get the kettle on," Mavis announced playfully digging Harold in the ribs, indicating he should get up. Kissing Mavis again he reluctantly obeyed. Groping in the dark for the large plastic torch, that had landed on the floor along with the clock. It was cold, much colder than it had been. Almost constant rain for the last three weeks had kept the temperature mild for the time of year. Now with the clocks going back an hour tomorrow night, Mother Nature had decided that a stiff frost was in order.

Mavis reached up and tried to wipe the usual coating of condensation from the window. She was surprised to find the hard cold icy coating that now covered the inside of the glass.

"Oh! It looks like Jack Frost has paid us a visit." She said surprised. Harold had finally found the torch, sending a shaft of bright light towards the seating end of the van. Their steamy breath, making the light dance as it rose haphazardly through the beam.

"Bugger it!" Harold snapped when his toe connected with the drop leg of the bed while searching for his thick dressing gown. Finally finding it hidden at the end of the bed, where it had fallen during their lovemaking.

Practised sweeps of the torch identified the gas lighter, on the small shelf next to the built-in gas fire. Harold lit the gas with practised ease, quickly moving through to the kitchen. Seconds passed as the gas-mantle slowly brightened, illuminating the small kitchen area that formed the front end of the twenty-two-foot van.

The little draining board had been cleared the night before ready for the morning ritual. The van had no toilet facilities, so washing had to be done in the tiny round sink. A pail, hidden under the work surface sufficed for relieving one's self during the night. Or first thing on a cold morning.

Harold opened the cupboard door and proceeded to pee into the half hidden plastic bucket, amidst a cloud of rising steam. More pressing requirements would have to wait until he habitually visited the small wooden shed where the chemical toilet was kept. The nature of Harold's job meant working in areas where there were no facilities at all. Experience made it good practice to make sure there would be no need of them during the day.

As usual, Mavis had seen to it that the two kettles were filled and sat on the small cooker, ready for the gas to be lit. That way should there be a stiff frost, freezing the water can; they would still have water in the kettles ready to heat. The small kettle held just enough for both of them to have a cup of tea. The big one contained enough water for first Harold them Mavis to have their morning wash. The little gas burner would labour to heat the big kettle, giving its sibling time to boil, brew the tea, and let them share breakfast, before boiling.

Harold suspected that it was warmer inside the little gas-fridge than in the kitchen. He retrieved the milk, butter, sugar, and bread. Taking them through to the table that occupied the space between the two bench couches, built into the far end of the van. Placing his burden on the table then lighting the two gas mantles, one either side of the area. Heat from the radiant glow of the gas fire was beginning to build up the expanding metal of the fire and flue creating a comforting, tick, tick, tick sound as the cold metal expanded.

Harold sat down and rolled a cigarette while waiting for the little kettle to come to the boil. He sat watching Mavis, who had pulled the blankets tightly around her head, the white sheet making her look like a nun. It was obvious that she was still revelling in the afterglow of their early morning passion. Mavis would wait till her tea was poured and the room had heated up a bit before leaving the comfort of the thick blankets.

"Have you thought of a name yet?" Harold asked thoughtfully.

"No, I thought we would leave it to nearer the time, you know after it's born." Mavis smiled, teasing,

"If it's a boy, we'll call him Harold, after you and your father." Harold frowned.

"Not bloody likely. Five generations of Harold's are enough for this family. No, If it's a boy, I would like him to be called Daniel." Mavis thought for a moment, then agreed.

"Okay, Daniel it is." She was surprised, that the decision had been so easy. Some of the other wives had spent months driving their husbands up the wall trying to pick names for their expected offspring. She liked it. It had a nice biblical ring.

"And if it's a girl?" She asked, a mischievous grin on her face. Harold paused ignoring the whistle from the small kettle as it came to the boil.

"Danielle. Yes. Danielle. If it's good enough for our son, then it will be good enough for our daughter." He answered rising to quiet the scream now emanating from the small kettle.

"And if its twins?" Mavis shouted through, giggling. Bursting into laughter as Harold's head snapped around the partition. A look of absolute bewilderment on his face.

Mavis was still laughing when Harold returned with the china teapot. Placing it on the woollen base and deftly slipping the brightly coloured woollen tea cosy over the bulbous china vessel.

He sat down, realizing that Mavis was pulling his leg.

"You know my mum told me that identical twins run in our family." Now Mavis looked shocked.

"Oh!" She said.

"In that case, we'll have to buy two of everything." Her eyes twinkling.

Harold knew that look. Mavis loved shopping, she would catch the train into the local town and spend the day roaming around, looking for the best bargains. Harold's meagre wage only allowed them to save a shilling or two each month. So far there was around fifty pounds in their savings account. Quite a feat for a woman who had to work on six pounds a week. Wherever possible clothes were mended, rather than buy new ones. Mavis was an excellent cook, always managing to put a good meal down for her man each night. Often denying herself a meal during the day. Both knew that would have to change. Mavis was now eating for two, or if her mischievous jibe had been correct, three. They sat sipping tea in silence, the only sound, a soft hiss from the gas fire, and the rhythmic ticking of Harold's old alarm clock. Both sat happily contemplating how their lives were going to change over the ensuing years.

Several weeks before the regional manager had asked Harold if he would take on a squad of his own. It would mean him coming down onto the ground after four years climbing. The pay increase would certainly be needed, now that Mavis was pregnant.

"You know you're not the only one with news," Harold announced, waiting for her response.

"Well, spill it." She answered impatiently.

"You know Mike Simpson, the regional manager?" She nodded,

"Well, he came looking for me last week. Offered me a squad of my own." Mavis throttled the excitement trying to burst out. Answering calmly.

"What did you say?" Harold frowned; knowing that what he was about to say would not go well with Mavis.

"I told him I wasn't interested." He held up his hand stopping her retort, hurt at the look of disappointment that washed over her thin face.

"Maybe I should get Pat to give him a call later. Tell him I've changed my mind." This was a surprise; Harold's love of climbing was the only thing Mavis wanted to change. Each day when he left she sat and uttered a silent prayer, willing him to come home safely that night.

Unable to hide her pleasure Mavis jumped around the table and hugged her partner. Showering him with kisses as the big kettle started to whistle.

"You go and get washed and I'll look out that new warn gear I bought for you during the summer." Again, she kissed him and wiggled her way out from behind the table, dragging him along behind her. Harold squeezed past, taking just that bit longer to pass, responding to the pressure from her bottom as she pushed it against him. Happily, pleased with the resulting bulge in his pyjamas.

Harold growled, shaking himself. Mavis was hard to deny. Nevertheless, if he didn't get a move on Pat would be round knocking at the door. Reluctantly he pulled away from her and headed for the small kitchen. First things first. The shed called.

Chapter 2. The Shed.

Harold picked up the big plastic torch and opened the caravan door. Allowing an icy wall of air to enter the van. With practised ease, he slipped out and closed the door. His slippers crunching on the frosty path. The padlock on the shed still soaking from three weeks of rain had frozen, denying him entry to the interior of the shed. It was almost a full minute before the warmth of his hand transferred enough heat to free the damp mechanism. Leaving the palm of his left hand cold and wet. The extended wait was also allowing the cold to permeate through the thick dressing gown and pyjamas.

Normally he would switch on the small battery light and read absent-mindedly through the old catalogue that hung beside the chemical toilet. This morning he was content to sit in the darkness, contemplating the changes that were about to overtake them. The plastic seat was cold and wet on his bare backside, taking several minutes longer than usual to come up to body-heat.

He had a feeling that his mother would be pleased, his father ecstatic. Finally, the old man would have an excuse to get him to give up the job he loved, and force him to re-join the family business. Harold frowned at the thought. His father had been a baker to trade until years of handling flower had become too much for his skin. dermatitis had made it impossible for him to run the small, one-man shop that kept the village going with bread and rolls. So the old man had turned to his real first love, growing things.

The old boy spent most of his spare time on his allotment, growing vegetables for the shop. during the war, he had made a tidy profit selling the fruits of his labours during the years when meat was rationed. It was the vegetables that had helped them get through the lean time, during and after the war. Harold had been six when the war started in 1939.

The small village of Newmains had been a model similar to the village of New-Lanark. Built in the early 19th century by some English gentleman who had decided to develop the rich coal and iron reserves in the area. The village was built to house the employees for the mines and Iron-works. Harold remembered standing on top of the slag-bing that separated the villages of Bonkle and Newmains. As a young boy, he had looked around his domain, building a mental map of the area, places to explore, things to see, etc.

Now the prospect of returning home had only one colour; Grey. Even now twenty-four years on since that first exploration to the summit of the slag-bing. The village was still grey with the fall-out from the blast furnaces and the adjoining foundry. In his recollections, even the people were grey. In Harold's mind even, the green vegetables that his old man grew, were grey. The prospect of returning home to daily battles with the old man was not one he was like to dwell on.

The baker's shop had been sold-on in 1948 when his dad's skin condition made it impossible to continue. The old man had bought 14 acres of land and turned it into a fairly successful small-holding. Content to spend the rest of his life growing vegetables for the local grocer's shops. A nice idea, but the reality was slightly different. Freed from the constraints of the shop, the old-man was apt to wander, making excuses that he had to run an errand or had to see someone about something-or-other. Leaving Harold to do the donkey work. Over the years this had driven a wedge between father and son. Oh, the old man wasn't lazy by any measure; he just tended to wander at the wrong times.

National service had given Harold a chance to escape from the steadily greying world of his childhood. Given half a chance he would have stayed on in the army. Had it not been for two unconnected events separated by half a world. First, he had been stationed in Malaya. More suited to the colder climate of Scotland Harold had contracted dysentery and was taken off active duty. At home, his mother had badly injured her hand in an accident with a carving knife. Rendering the two strong workforces on the small-holding, one-half short. His father had taken advantage of both events and applied for a dispensation to have Harold released from national service early. The authorities agreed, and he had been shipped home.

The old man was happy, his son was at home where there wasn't any danger of him being shot or contracting some exotic disease and dying on foreign shores. While on the other hand, Harold was becoming increasingly restless. A chance encounter with a local motor engineer brought the prospect of an apprenticeship. It had caused another major row with the old man, but with his mother's help he had finally won out. He still worked on the smallholding in the evenings and at weekends. Enjoying the freedom from his father that working on cars gave him.

Even then the old man had managed to win out in the end. A hernia, the product of carrying twenty-stone bags of flour as an apprentice baker, had returned. Rendering the old man useless for over a year. Harold had been forced to leave his job as a mechanic and return to the small-holding, on the promise that he would be allowed to finish his apprenticeship when his father recovered.

In the late fifties, Harold still trapped in the now failing family business had met Mavis. She had been holidaying with an aunt who lived on one of the large estates on Clyde-side. Harold had been sent to pick-up some bales of peat with the old VW pickup. A welcome escape brought about by the old man's inability to lift the heavy and cumbersome objects.

Mavis and her cousin had been sitting on the stone step of the farmhouse sunning themselves and drinking home-made lemonade. The demands of work had left little time in Harold's life for socializing. Preferring tinkering with his old Austin 7 to spending hours in the pub.

Harold had become a recluse since returning home from Malaya. He'd seen the two girls sitting on the step when he pulled into the yard. Alison, he knew and had little time for. However, the dark slim one was a stranger. distracted, by the girls on the step he nearly rammed the old pick-up into the wall of the close. Just managing to stop the vehicle inches from the red sandstone wall of a barn. Unaware of his near miss He reversed the pickup across the close and stopped short of a large open doorway.

Mesmerised Harold sat for a moment staring at the young woman, sitting happily enjoying her lemonade. dressed in a simple summer dress, which complimented her short curly dark hair. She was sitting leaning forward onto her crossed legs, sipping her lemonade through a straw, her foot swinging rhythmically in time to some unknown beat. Her feet were bare, shoes discarded, letting the back and forth movement cool her small but shapely foot.

Alison nudged her with her shoulder, sending both girls into fits of giggles. Mavis blushed and dropped her head, trying to hide her embarrassment from the handsome stranger. Both girls continued to giggle as he jumped out of the pick-up and made his way into the shed. The old man had seen to the purchase of the bales during the winter, and an arrangement had been made to store them in this barn until they were required. This would be the third and final load that year, precluding any further visits to the estate. Something would have to be done, and quickly if he was to become acquainted with this unknown young woman.

It would take a good twenty minutes to load the pickup, first, he had to throw five, or six bales onto the truck then jump up and stack them two deep, before returning to the shed to repeat the process. On his second foray onto the truck he observed that Alison had disappeared, leaving the other girl on her own. She appeared to be watching him.

He returned to the building, worried that she also would have disappeared, next time he climbed onto the truck. In his haste, he picked up the 12-stone bale of peat and easily launched it through the door, towards the pick-up. The bale sailed through the wide opening, narrowly missing the slender silhouette of a young woman, entering the dark barn.

"Look-out!" Harold shouted, as the big bale flashed by the girl, who had seen the on-coming projectile and neatly sidestepped, allowing the tightly packed lump of peat to flash safely past. Landing on the back of the truck, right where Harold had intended.

He rushed towards Mavis, terrified that the big bale had hit her. His foot caught on one of the wooden slats wired around the peat to help keep the bales square. Fate intervened, placing Mavis right in front of Harold as he fell. The net result was Mavis landed on her back with a very embarrassed Harold on top of her. Both stared into the eyes of the other for what seemed like an age until finally, Mavis started to giggle. Breaking the ice. Harold succumbed to the comedy of the situation, burying his head in her shoulder in an attempt to stifle his own laughter.

Mavis was impressed; Harold had a very well developed and muscular body. While he had been pleasantly surprised by the impression that Mavis's slim but perfectly proportioned physique was making on him. He was speechless, his tongue tied in knots. Moving would mean having to face the young woman eye to eye.

Sitting there in the dark shed, the memories of his first encounter with Mavis made him chuckle. When finally, they had both got to their feet. All he had been able to say was,

"I'll pick you up at seven, then?"

Brushing the last of the dry peat from her dress, Mavis smiled and simply said,

"Ok. Oh, by the way. I'm Mavis."

"Ha-Harold." He stammered.

"I know. See you at seven then." Then she turned and walked out of the barn, squeezing past the sides of the old VW. Silhouetting her tidy frame against the bright yard.

Chapter 3. The Four Tonner.

Somewhere in the distance, Harold could hear Pat starting the ex-army Bedford 4-tonner that they used to run the gang to the sites. He must have been sitting longer than usual. Tearing a page from the catalogue, Harold cleaned himself then dropped a woollen jumper over the lid. It would keep the frost off the seat for Mavis when she ventured out to the shed later.

Outside the stars reminded him of glow-worms he'd seen when he was stationed in Malaya. He paused, studying the bright points of light in the sky, before deciding that the only stars that really mattered were Mavis and the child she was carrying. Whatever it's sex.

A wall of warm damp air greeted Harold as he opened the caravan door. It was one of the eccentricities of a mobile life. While the thin walls would bleed heat to the atmosphere fairly quickly when the fire was turned off, it would heat up just as quickly when the fire was turned on. By the time Harold re-entered the van the temperature had risen to a comfortable fifty degrees, still cold by house standards but comfortable for seasoned caravan dwellers. Harold loved the warm-moist atmosphere that the gaslights and fire produced, especially in cold weather. There was a quality to the air that just made him feel warm.

Mavis had filled the little sink with from the kettle. Now the water was just at the right temperature. Harold stripped down and began to wash, using nothing more than a flannel face cloth and soap. Mavis assisted, washing his back, then rubbed him down with a large bath-towel. Neither spoke much, enjoying the intimate contact and each other's company while they could.

"I've laid out your new clothes on the bed, lover." She said finally satisfied that he had dried himself properly.

"There are new underpants, vest, long-Johns, mole-skins, jumper, and socks. You should put on the new donkey jacket and wellies Pat gave you the other day. Oh, and I got you new dungarees." Mavis retrieved the heavy cotton garment from the bottom of the small wardrobe that marked the separation between the mid-section of the van, and the seating area.

Harold's practised ear, recognised the sound of the Four-Toners cold gearbox whining, as Pat made his way slowly up through the twisted roads that wound through the caravan site. He would be trying to steer the cumbersome truck with only limited visibility. during the summer the old-bugger had a habit of boiling over, so Pat had asked him to remove the thermostat. Now in the colder air of late autumn, he would probably have to put it back. Even hammering the old beast down the narrow lanes wouldn't get the heater going. The only way to get the windscreen clear was to open both side windows in an attempt to equalize the temperature between the cab and the outside.

Harold finished dressing, finally pulling on the new donkey jacket. The new wellies felt strange, slightly tight with the new thick and fluffy woollen socks inside. No doubt in a few days they would settle down. Harold always felt strange in new clothes.

"I feel like I'm dressed for a funeral Mave." He whined like a young child forced to go to school with a brand-new uniform. She smiled, stretching up on her tiptoes, and pulling him down at the same time, kissing him playfully on the cheek.

"Go on out with you, you naughty boy. Or you'll be late for school." She chided, mockingly. Wagging her finger in front of his face the way his mother used to do when he was a child. Harold made a mock attempt to bite her out-stretched finger. Snapping his teeth shut just short of her finger-tip. While whining softly like a playful puppy.

"Do I have too?" he said, pleadingly as Mavis handed him his knapsack.

"See you tonight lover-boy. There's Pat." Mavis had heard the Big Irishman's footfall on the gravel strip between the tarmac road, and the concrete plot that the van sat on. Sure enough. As Harold reached the door, Pat's huge knuckles rapped the metal coated door. Mavis had always thought Pat had the knock of a policeman.

"Yu dare Harry?" He called as Harold opened the door.

"Got any cardboard we can put down in front of the radiator?" Mavis and Pat waved to each other. Mavis knew that the minute her man stepped through the door, he passed into another world.

Gone was the playful, caring, kind and considerate lover, who would do anything for her. Harold had now joined the ranks of the working man. In its place a skilled and confident climber, who also had a gift for all things mechanical. He would be that way until around seven o'clock in the evening when he climbed in the door and shed his working clothes. The rigours of the day evaporating as each garment was removed and discarded on the tiny kitchen floor.

"In the shed," Harold answered, reaching back inside, removing the silver padlock key from the hook above the door where it normally hung, ready for instant use. The door closed. Harold and Pat became muffled voices, rummaging through the junk at the back of the little shed. Mavis returned to the table, pouring herself a last cup of tea from the still warm pot.

Harold secured a large flattened cardboard box from the jumble at the back of the shed.

"I think this will do Pat." He said handing the object out to the big Irishman. Whilst doing his best to return some sort of order to the chaos he had created while recovering the box. Pat, as always impatient to get on, took the box and headed for the truck, which sat idling in the railway station car park, just outside the site gate.

By the time Harold reached the truck Pat had almost finished securing the cardboard to the flat front of the old Bedford. Carefully leaving around four inches at the bottom to allow some cold air to pass through the massive radiator.

"What's with the new gear?" Pat asked, using an old penknife to cut the trailing ends of the hemp strands he had used to tie the cardboard to the grill.

"Got some good news this morning. Mave's pregnant." Harold answered while picking up the debris from the ganger's hurried repairs. Pat was always in a hurry. Even when there was only one short job to do, he would hound them on to get it finished. The flip side of the coin was that when all the work was completed, they would be allowed to sit around and chew-the-fat.

"Congratulations. When is she due?"

"March, I think. I'll know better tonight. How's the time?" Answered Harold as he stowed his knap-sack behind the wooden driver's seat. Before Pulling himself up, and expertly inserting himself behind the wheel.

"Ten to seven. Let's get on." Pat was anxious to get moving. Fortunately, the cardboard had done the trick, a damp area was beginning to form at the bottom of the driver's windscreen just above the vent. With luck by the time they managed the two miles or so to the main road the window should be clear. For the moment he would have to content himself with wiping the mist from the inside. Pat had scraped the frost from the outside before starting the engine.

Still, the narrow lanes were a trial for the old truck at the best of times. Geared down for army convoy speeds, the truck could only manage around twenty miles per hour. As even the massive steering wheel wasn't enough to overcome the slow and sometimes extremely heavy steering. Harold had an advantage over the rest of the gang. He had been a driver of this very same model during his national service. The key to keeping the heavy steering supple was grease. Lots and lots of it. All the track ends and especially the stub-pins had to be done regularly, otherwise in dry or cold weather the old grease congealed and actually worked to increase the effort required to turn the truck.

As a force of habit Harold had seen to it the truck received a good greasing at least twice a week. Even Pat had marvelled at the difference in the old machine. Prior to Harold joining the gang the ancient truck had been abused and neglected. It broke down regularly, causing no end of delays.

Pat had reluctantly given into Harold's insistence that he be allowed time on the truck. The results had been instantaneous, first and most importantly, the trucks brakes now worked in the way that they should. Previous attempts at stopping the vehicle had been risky at best. Hills had become a major hazard. The vehicle had to be stopped at the top, a low gear engaged then the driver would gingerly move off hoping that the engine-braking would be enough to stop the old machine from careering out of control. Meeting a car on one of the narrow twisting lanes, that often-had steep hills, usually resulted in them taking out many yards of the roadside hedge. It was a good thing that the British army insisted that their vehicles were capable of the very sort of abuse that this type of incident involved.

In an attempt to ensure some sort of stopping power Pat had the leaver that engaged the four-wheel-drive welded in place. This had two effects. One, the only remaining working brake, spread its effort through the drive train, at least until it locked up. An event that required the driver using the big steering wheel as an anchor while pressing with all his strength on the pedal. Stopping the vehicle in this manner had become a problem as all the strain was put onto a single set of brake shoes.

The second was that the truck tended to wear tyres down very quickly. Blow-outs were a regular occurrence. On Harold's first day with the gang, the offside front tyre had blown as Pat pushed the truck around a sharp left-hand bend at full-throttle. The old machine had heeled over, crossing the narrow lane, mounting the three-foot-high verge and sailing out through a six-foot beach hedge before coming to rest in a field of turnips.

It was a miracle that no-one had been hurt. Harold had set about giving the huge Irishman a piece of his mind. Insisting that he be allowed to look after the vehicle. Reluctantly Pat agreed. Harold spent the next four hours doing makeshift repairs on the truck while they waited for the fitter to bring out a new wheel. As usual, the spare was flat.

When the fitter arrived, the truck was already blocked up, the old wheel removed, ready for the new one to be bolted on. Harold had borrowed a grease gun and some grease from the fitter and set-about lubricating the steering while the rest of the gang had assisted the mechanic to refit the new wheel. Both whining front and back differentials and a dry gearbox had been topped up with oil. A borrowed hacksaw removed the link locking the transmission in four-wheel drive.

When the blocks were removed, Harold jumped into the driver's seat and easily drove the truck back out through the hole in the hedge, ignoring the muddy conditions in the field. Pat had been insistent that they would need a tractor to pull the truck out of the field, which would have meant waiting for another hour or two for one of the companies' heavy county four-wheel drive tractors could make its way to them.

Harold had been the first man to stand up to Pat. The big Irishman's size coupled with his habitual foul temper usually guaranteed that his will was absolute. Harold had not only stood up to Pat's attempt to shout him down but had deflected the ganger's anger away from the rest of the squad. The good-natured Scotsman had calmed the innate foreman. Harold even had him laughing and cracking jokes while they waited for the fitter to bring the new wheel.

Later that day when they finally got to the site, Harold's confident, and methodical climbing abilities had further strengthened his position with the big Irishman, guaranteeing him a place in the squad. That had been four years ago. during this time the two men and their families had become close.

Chapter 4. Rooster.

Fifteen minutes later Harold turned right onto the main road. Not all the gang lived in caravans. Two of the single men preferred to live in digs. Usually selecting accommodation near to or in a pub. Enjoying the social atmosphere that such lodgings allowed. Rooster, a tall, skinny red-haired idiot from Liverpool had taken lodgings in a pub called The Severed Head. It was the centre of a small hamlet even more remote than the one Harold and Pat had chosen to live near.

Two days later he had been asked to move out by the landlord. Thirty seconds after he found Rooster in bed with his 16-year-old daughter. Pat had acted quickly finding digs in a small boarding house much nearer Harold and himself. The new landlady was in her seventies, and none of the residents was at all interested in getting into bed with Rooster. Well, none of the female guests.

Roosters new lodgings were on the main road fifty yards from the junction with the lane to the village. As the truck turned out onto the road, Harold spotted Rooster standing by the lodging house gate. Illuminated by the weak headlights of the truck, Rooster resembled a scarecrow left out in a field for many years.

Harold pulled the truck to a halt, allowing Rooster to climb in over Pat. Settling himself on the heavily insulated engine cover.

"You been in the pub last night?" growled Pat as the smell of stale beer drifted towards him each time Rooster opened his mouth. The young man merely belched further polluting the cab with the odour of stale bitter. Pat shook his head and jibed,

"That fat little queer been trying to get up your arse again, boy?" Rooster nodded.

"You know one of these days your dangerous little game will have that little runt adjusting your piles, from the inside." The big Irishman seemed amused at the thought.

"Mind you if he gets a look at that dong between your legs, the poor little bugger will have a heart attack."

"Fuck off dick!" Answered Rooster, adjusting himself on the warming engine cover. His head hurt, and his mouth felt like a dry salt-bed. As usual, his retort was like a gun being fired. Short and sharp. Pat and Harold laughed; both knew Rooster had an intense hatred of queers. They also knew his love of alcohol, sometimes got the better of his judgement.

His evening ritual never changed. Harold would drop him off at the nearest village pub, and then he and Pat took the truck back to the caravan site. Rooster would enter the pub and drink 8 pints of bitter, no more, no less, before staggering back to his lodgings. Even well pickled, the scrawny Liverpudlian always made it home. Where he would peacefully make his way to bed then fall fast asleep. His landlady would wake him around 6:30, and insist that he washed and shaved before sitting down to breakfast.

Orphaned at the age of five Rooster had only known children's homes and foster parents. In a way, things hadn't changed. Landladies all over the country mothered the scurrilous rogue. At work, he had a lightning-quick logic that seemed to bypass all reason. By contrast, he was viewed as the resident idiot. More because of his abrupt delivery than any lack of intelligence. On the ground his hands shook constantly, 100 feet up on the pylon he had nerves of iron, easily walking along the 4-inch steel angles without care or worry. He and Harold were widely recognised as the top erection team in the company, holding the record for the most number of successful lifts in a day.

Harold's pleasant nature was in total contrast to Roosters aggressive abruptness. Pat had often commented on the differences that made the two of them gel when they were aloft. Rooster was in-fact the only one Pat had ever seen that could rile Harold, sometimes bringing the muscular Scotsman within a hairs-breadth of throttling his work-mate.

Pat often marvelled at the self-control Harold would bring to bear, especially when Rooster insinuated that he had been having sex with Mavis. They all knew that it was impossible including Harold. Somehow the idiot would niggle away at him until finally, he would touch a raw nerve. As it happened Roosters other great talent was his prowess as a sprinter. Easily out-distancing the heavier man. Fortunately for Rooster Harold never held a grudge for long, calming down quickly.

Someone had commented that it was the aggression between the two men on the ground that allowed them to work so well when climbing. In the two years, the two had been aloft together Pat had never heard a bad word between them. On the ground separating them was almost a daily event.

"Move your leg," Harold shouted at Rooster, trying to make himself heard over the noisy old engine. Rooster had placed his foot between the long straight gear-stick and the engine-cowling, preventing Harold from selecting third gear. As usual, Rooster failed to oblige, howling as Harold mashed the stick into gear, jamming roosters foot. Pat intervened,

"Rooster if you try that trick again, I'll throw you in the back and you can freeze your fucking bollocks off." Roosters retort was almost instantaneous.

"Tell this mad Jock bastard, to get off my back. You never blame him it's always me!" Now Pat was getting riled.

"You did that on purpose you scouse eejit, and I'm not in the mood for your shenanigans, this morning. One more word and Wing-nut will be riding shotgun on that warm engine cover. "Get me?" Pat emphasised his displeasure by hauling Rooster into a sitting position banging his head on the rusted inside of the cab."

"What you do that for you fucking mad Irish bastard?" Rooster howled, angrily, rubbing his forehead just where the short curly red hair stopped.

Harold stayed out of it. Roosters, attempt at winding him up had forced him to mash the long gear-stick into position. Unfortunately, years of miss-use had worn the selectors to the point where, if not handled correctly, the old truck would lock into third gear. It was geared to high to pick away easily and too low to manage anything other than 10 miles per hour without the engine roaring its head off.

One of the reasons that Pat insisted Harold drove the old truck was his skill and intimate knowledge of this particular model. Harold's regular maintenance prevented most of the stupid breakdowns that had occurred before he joined the gang. Gear-jamming had been a regular occurrence, Pat's impatience had tended to force the gear-changes rather than give them the time that Harold did by instinct.

During Pat's term as the driver the truck rarely travelled at any more than 10 miles per hour. The problem was relatively easy to cure by removing eighteen five-sixteenth bolts that held the top cover onto the gearbox, then slip it to the side by using a large screwdriver as a leaver. A quick flick and the selector would be free then replace the cover and tighten the bolts. Fifteen minutes in total would fix the problem. However, first, they would have to stop. Second, it was still dark. Third, the rest of the gang would be waiting for them eight miles further down the road.

Harold lifted his foot, allowing the roaring engine to quieten enough to let Pat hear him.

"You want me to stop and fix it, Pat?" The big Irishman still held Rooster by the lapels of his worn donkey jacket, Glaring at the stupid grin on Roosters acne-studded face. However, Rooster wasn't finished yet. He produced a loud and stinking belch right into Pats face driving Pat's anger to new heights. The move was carefully calculated to hold them up. If Harold stopped, they would be on their way again in about quarter of an hour. Arriving on site only a few minutes late. On the other hand, if they didn't stop, it would take twice the time to cover the eight miles to the next pick-up, and another full hour to get to the site. Allowing Rooster to fall asleep on top of the warm engine cover.

"No, keep the fucker going. This bastard will have to work twice as hard today, to make up time." Pat shouted back, releasing the drunken fool pushing him back down, causing him to bang the back of his head this time. Fortunately, Rooster had a thick skull.

Chapter 5. Running Repairs.

Forty minutes later Harold pulled the truck to a halt outside The Pig and Whistle, which sat right in the middle of a small hamlet called Easter Mingthorpe. One of the many rural English villages that had so-far escaped the developments threatening to disrupt rural life in the mid-twentieth century. The village had one claim to fame, three street-lights. One either side of the pub, and one at the end of the lane leading down to the caravan site at the edge of the village. The village shop and post office sat on the corner of this lane, hence the need for a third street-lamp. The tiny school which had a population of around fifty children sat on the other side of the narrow street.

The street-light had been put there to aid the children crossing the road on the dark winter mornings. A good proportion of whom came from the fifty odd families who permanently lived in the caravan site. Other than the bus stop and the twenty or so picturesque cottages, there was nothing else of note in the hamlet.

By the time Harold pulled up outside the Pig and Whistle, Pat was ready to murder Rooster. The lad's basic diet of bacon and eggs followed by his nightly eight pints of bitter habitually produced a devastating smell when he farted. Every two or three minutes Rooster would silently push one out, filling the cab with the foulest smell imaginable. Harold had dropped the window in his door. Allowing freezing air to enter the cabin in an attempt to dilute the odour. Pat wasn't as lucky. His window had been jammed in place after Rooster had broken the thick leather strap that held the window up. Even Rooster, who was trying his best to make light of the situation, by giving each one a rating out of ten, had to admit, that today he was especially putrid. He howled with delight each time Pat roared at him.

Still Pat wouldn't let Harold stop. Instead, threatening Rooster with ever greater ladles of punishment. Finally, when Harold drew the truck to a halt, Pat opened the door and almost fell out of the cabin in his haste to get away from the nose-wrinkling odour. Harold had exited from the driver's side of the cab, unable to make up his mind whether to choke on the smell or choke with laughter at the expression on Pat's face. The last of Rooster's little bombs had been especially devastating. Rooster jumped nonchalantly from the cab, content that he had managed to inflict some form of revenge for the two bumps on the head Pat had given him earlier.

He would happily spend the rest of the journey in the back of the truck with the rest of the gang now that he had successfully put one over on the big Irishman. Unfortunately, the foul smell had the capability to linger on after Rooster had left. Even though The gangly Liverpudlian had vacated the cab, Pat and Harold's ordeal wasn't over yet. Grudgingly Pat gave in to Harold's request to repair the gearbox selector.

Pat knew about Mike Simpson's offer to give Harold a squad of his own. He was happy for his friend. Harold was very capable of running a gang. The big problem had always been his reluctance to accept responsibility. Gaining promotion wasn't a case of if he was capable; it was more about finally accepting the inevitable, and giving into the repeated requests.

On the way to pick-up Rooster, Harold had asked him to call Mike Simpson, to ask if the post was still open. Pat already knew the answer. He had been talking with the area manager the previous weekend. Yes, the post was still open, and he had asked Pat to encourage Harold to take it. Now needing time to cool off from Rooster's odorous attack on the way to Easter Mingthorpe. Pat decided to let Harold get the gearbox fixed, not by doing it himself, but by instructing one of the other men. A gaffer must be able to delegate. To stand back and let someone else make an utter cock-up of it without losing your own head. Unlike himself!

"Harry, get the men to sort the gearbox while I take Rooster for a little walk." Harold nodded, laughing as Rooster launched himself from the relative safety of the back of the truck. Pat merely reached up and caught Roosters donkey jacket as he attempted to escape. Hauling the struggling Liverpudlian to his feet with one massive Irish hand.

"You're coming with me, you little runt!" Pat's growled words, moulded Roosters pockmarked face into a mask of fear. Pat held his face inches from his own, glaring menacingly into the Liverpudlian's eyes, an evil smile forming on his lips. Rooster now worried belched once more, causing Pat's nose to twitch. Seconds later the ganger disappeared around the side of the pub, dragging the terrified Rooster behind.

The rest of the eight-man squad had been waiting for the truck to arrive. None of them was very happy to be left hanging around in the cold. Especially when it became apparent that Rooster had done it again. All five of them smiled as Pat disappeared around the side of the pub, gleefully dragging a terrified and reticent Rooster behind him.

"What did the little bastard do this time Harry?" Asked Di Jones, one of the two Welsh winch-men. Both named David Jones. One from Swansea, the other from Abervan. A system had been worked out that managed to dispel any confusion about which one was being addressed. The one from Abervan was referred to as Di Jones, and the other as Davie Jones. Di operated the main winch while Davie; the more senior of the two operated the control winch. Which was by far the more skilled of the two jobs.

"Have a whiff of that Di." Harold answered thumbing in the direction of the open cab door.

"Good god Harry, how did you manage to stand it?" There was humour in the Welshman's melodious tones.

"With difficulty. Wing-nut, can you jump up and clear the front of the bed. We need to get the hatch above the gearbox open. Davie, would you get my toolbox from under Pat's seat. Take the cover off the top of the gearbox and lever the selector back into place. You two make sure Wing-nut doesn't tangle your slings." There was an unspoken rule in the squad that placed Harold in charge when Pat wasn't there. Over the preceding years the men, with the exception of Rooster, had developed a deep respect for the good-natured Scotsman.

Chapter 6. Wing-nut.

At nineteen Wing-nut, was the youngest of the crew, joining just after his eighteenth birthday. He was the gopher and general dogs-body. Tall and gangly like Rooster, but there the similarities ended. He was a plodder; outwardly content to do whatever the men asked of him. Unfortunately, nature had blessed him with a pair of huge ears that stuck straight out, a weak chin and a long thin protruding nose. His miss-fortune was further compounded by a childhood break, that had left the last quarter of the misshapen proboscis twisted down and to his left.

Like Rooster Wing-nut preferred to live in digs. Not being a drinker, living in a pub caused few problems for the beanpole from Hale in Cornwall. Preferring his own company, the quiet lad was actually a closet genius. At school, he had been ridiculed because of his over-sized ears and misshaped face. Unlike most of the boys, he wasn't fated to become a fisherman. His father had the dubious position of sergeant in the local constabulary, making his life even harder. In essence, he had been an outcast. Bullied and shunned by almost all of his contemporise, he had developed a taste for knowledge.

Books had become his diversion from the pains of every-day life. In the beginning, it had been comics, lots, and lots of comics. His mother had fallen ill when he was only six. With his father working odd shifts, the young Gerald had spent most of his time by his mother's bedside where they would listen to plays on the wireless. It had been his job to change stations on the big wooden radio that sat on top of his mother's ornate chest of drawers.

The delicately carved piece had been lovingly produced in India by a master craftsman, sometime in the late eighteen hundred's. It had been specially commissioned by his great-grandfather as a wedding present for his new wife before they returned home from India. The intricate carvings on either side mirrored each other in all but gender, female on the right and male on the left. The drawer fronts had been in-laid with different polished woods; even the blades of elephant grass had been painstakingly reproduced with slivers of bamboo. Exotic animals populated the jungle clearing between the two figures. It was rumoured that they were supposed to bring prosperity to the newly-weds. Perhaps they would have done so had the couple stayed in India.

Soon after their return to England, a failed investment had stripped the couple of all financial assets. It was ironic that the very symbol of prosperity was, in fact, the only thing left after the creditors had finished. It was only years later that his great-grandmother had learned that the piece had never actually been paid for. Being a straight-laced and very honest woman, she had seen their miss-fortune as punishment for her husband's ill deeds. On her death she had passed the instrument of her shame onto her daughter, stating that they should keep it as a warning to the consequences of dishonesty.

As a child when not listening to the radio, he would read to his mother. At first, he read his books from school. This constant exposure to literature soon pushed him well beyond the other members of his class. One of the greatest comforts of his life was the memory of his mother's passing. Her last breath was through smiling lips as he read aloud the closing sentence of Rudyard Kipling's Jungle Book.

Life had been hard for the boy after that. His father was strict, treating his son more like an errant constable than his only child. Life had been difficult. Gerald's only concession from his father had been a trip to the small local library. The old man had filled out the forms and paid the sixpence membership fee. That had been his eighth birthday present and the only really good thing his straight-laced father had done for him.

At the age of ten, his father had remarried. Elsie his stepmother had been good to him, taking him on as her own.

"What you reading lad?" she had asked one morning while standing at the big kitchen table rolling out dough for making pasties. Gerald had been sitting at the range enjoying the warmth of the open fire as he read a book on British butterflies.

"Oh, just stuff." Gerald had answered quietly, attempting to deflect her curiosity. He was afraid that the down to earth Elsie would have little time for him reading books on the local fauna.

However, she was not about to be deflected. Seconds later Gerald found floury fingers pushing the spine of the book forward so that she could see the book title.

"That's a good book, is that. My old mum let me read it when I was a young girl. She loved butterflies. We often walked across the moor trying to find some of the ones in the book. Found some of them too." Gerald had been so surprised; he just sat and stared at her with his mouth open.

Smiling she ignored his surprise and ploughed on.

"Your dad tells me you used to sit and read to your mother, God rest her soul. I never seem to get the time to read anymore. Would you like to read that book to me while I get on with these pasties?"

Elsie, it turned out had been a bookworm herself as a young woman, revelling in romantic fiction. However, the plump little woman maintained that if a story was worth writing, it must be worth reading, so she was prepared to listen to whatever it was he had to read. At first, it had been science fiction, which in turn generated an interest in science and mathematics. Later they found new worlds in classical works, Shakespeare, Homer, in-fact if it was between two book covers he read it for her.

Just shortly after his fifteenth birthday his father had contracted pneumonia and died leaving Gerald and Elsie alone and almost penniless. The boy had been forced to leave school and get a job on the fishing boats in order to try and make ends meet.

For three years they had managed to keep the wolf from the door. Elsie had taken in washing and repaired clothing while his job on the small fishing boats brought in some much-needed cash.

Then a chance meeting between Elsie and Pat's wife Marge at the local shop had opened up an opportunity. Pat's gang was in the area working on a new line of pylons that would bring power to Penzance. One of the men had quit opening up a job for a labourer. That evening Elsie, knowing how much Gerald hated working on the fishing boats told the boy about it. He had thought about it for a few seconds.

"If I got that job you'd be left alone here. I'll have to send money home each week." Elsie was surprised at the matter of fact answer. The gangly teenager had become a lot like his father as the years had marched on. The thought of him leaving home tore at her heart, almost as much as the thought of him being trapped in a job he hated.

"I'll be okay. The vicar's wife asked me if I'd do a couple of hours cleaning each week. Along with the washing and mending. I'll get by." And that was that. Later that evening they both walked to the caravan site.

Pat had been a bit reticent at first fearing that the lad's gangly appearance lacked the strength needed for the labouring job. Finally, he gave in, if Gerald didn't work out by the time they moved on to the next string, then the lad would stay at home. As it turned out the boy had a number of unsung talents that quickly made him part of the gang.

One turned out to be a near perfect memory which Pat used to great effect when Rooster was trying to pull a fast one on him. The boy had specific orders from his foreman, stick close, and listen to everything. No matter how small or seemingly insignificant, especially when strangers came on site. Years of running gangs had taught Pat one thing; everyone higher up the pecking order than him had selective memory and hearing. Wing-nut's photographic memory provided him with a method of levelling the playing field.

His oversized lobes had the side effect of channelling sound to his eardrums more efficiently than they would have had his ears been normal. Di and Davie Jones reckoned the lad could hear a pin drop into the mud at 100 yards in a thunderstorm.

Like most Welshmen, they both loved to sing, and it was quite normal to hear Men of Harlech or some other Welsh song drifting over the field around the erection site. How surprised they had been when a third voice joined in, matching them in precision and harmony. Wing-nut proved to be a powerful baritone that harmonised in nicely with the other two men.

With the exception of Rooster, all the men had developed a deep respect for Wing-nut's abilities, quickly accepting him as a member of the gang. The lad never used his talents to his own advantage, preferring to hide them behind his quiet stoicism and hard work. Even his nickname, given to him the first time Rooster had clapped eyes on him had become his accepted manner of address, using his given name only in quieter more intimate conversations. For the first time in his uncomfortable life, he was happy. His nickname wasn't the most complimentary, but to him, it had become his badge of acceptance.

Chapter 7. Davies' hand.

The coiled ropes in the back of the truck lay like potato slices each one half on top of the next lying between the benches that ran along both sides of the truck bed. This meant that all the ropes had to be lifted out before the hatch in the floor could be exposed. Fortunately, Wing-nut and the two Davies were well used to stacking and un-stacking the ropes. With the help of the two riggers, the operation took only a few minutes. Clearing the small wooden hatch resulted in an orderly pile of coiled ropes and boxes at the rear of the truck ready for systematic re-deployment back on the truck-bed once the gearbox had been fixed.

At Harold's suggestion, the men undid the ties holding the heavy canvas cover from the first three of five thick metal frames, allowing light from both street-lights to flood the back of the truck. As usual, the batteries in the big chrome torches were flat. Undaunted Davie Jones rummaged in Harold's toolbox, finally finding the large plain screwdriver he had been looking for. A few scrapes along the outline of the hatch pulled out most of the dirt that had accumulated in the crack. A few deft bangs', and the cover was easily levered off exposing the gearbox cover plate, just behind the point that the gear linkage disappeared into the top of the box.

A thick coating of dirt, thrown up from the front wheels each time the old four-wheel drive truck had been ploughing through mud, had to be chipped off with the screwdriver. Revealing the eighteen bolt-heads, Davie selected the appropriate half-inch drive socket from Harold's toolbox and quickly slackened each bolt. A change to the speed-brace, allowed him to run each bolt out quickly handing each to Wing-nut to place safely in a small box ready for re-assembly.

With the boy's aid, the top cover was lifted off and placed behind them.

"Okay, Harry we got the top off the box. What you want us to do now?" Davie called out to Harold.

"Can you see the selector yokes? They look like silver bars connected to forks. There should be two; one on the top gear set and one further down in the box."

"I see them, Harry."

"Take the screwdriver and lever the bottom one forward. It should go quite easily."

"I got it. It's dark in here. I will have to feel my way around to get the driver in place."

"Be careful Davie, don't get your hand caught in the cogs. There are a lot of sharp edges in there." Harold had made sure that the handbrake had been applied, before allowing anyone near the internal moving parts of the gearbox.

All of the men had moved to the back of the truck, listening intently to Harold's instructions. None noticed Rooster bolt from the far end of the Pig and Whistle and make for the relative safety of the cab with a very red-faced Pat close at his heels. Whatever had gone on behind the pub, Rooster seemed to be in fear of his life.

Yanking the door open Rooster hurriedly climbed into the cab, dragging the door shut behind him. Banging the lock pin down just as Pat grabbed the door handle. Too late the door swung open. Roosters face was white with shock; Pat had pulled the door so hard that the silver handle on the inside came off in Rooster's right hand.

Pat lunged for the open fronts of Roosters donkey jacket narrowly missing as the frightened scouser pulled back, banging hard against the long hand-brake lever. His shoulder knocked the latch, allowing the lever to spring forward. releasing the brake.

Kicking out at Pat, Rooster's wellie boot hit the starter button causing the starter to engage. Locked in third gear, all that happened was the truck lunged forward, then stopped as the starter motor disengaged. Davie Jones had dropped the screwdriver into the gearbox and was groping around in the dark trying to locate the thick handle. The sudden jerk through the drive train freed the locked selector fork, throwing it backwards, jamming Davie's hand, causing his fingers to be drawn between two lay-shafts. The Welshman howled, trying to pull his trapped hand free.

Harold realizing what had happened ran towards the cab, shouting to Wing-nut to keep Davie still. Arriving at the cab door to find Pat hauling a screaming Rooster out of the cab by the nuts a move that would have landed anyone else in a hospital. In Roosters case he had been rendered immune to such pain after a horrific kicking from a fellow inmate in one of the children's homes that he had grown up in. Now if kicked in the groin, he merely gave himself a shake and carried on as if nothing had happened. His incessant howling was more a plea for sympathy rather than the result of any real injury.

Harold's rush for the cab brought some sense to the enraged Irishman. At the sound of Davies painful screams, he unceremoniously dropped Rooster, leaving him, to tend to the injured man. Pat may have appeared rough and ready, but when it came to the safety of his men the Irish giant was years ahead of his time. Safety was paramount in the day-to-day operation of the gang. Because of this, potentially fatal accidents had been turned into a series of frightening near misses. Pat's gang had the best safety record in the company, in spite of the lack of anything more than basic safety equipment.

Within Seconds Harold had secured the handbrake, while Pat had jumped up onto the truck-bed, beside Davie. Wing-nut had grabbed Davies arm, trying to prevent him from pulling his injured hand free. The shock was beginning to set in, masking some of the pain and allowing Davie to be calmed.

"Get the torch from my bag, lad," Pat instructed Wing-nut, almost gently. "You hang in there Davie Jones. We'll have you out in no-time."

After securing the handbrake Harold rushed back to join Pat and the injured Welshman, muscling the others out of the way quickly joining Pat and the injured man. Harold arrived as Wing-nut swung round from the nearside door of the cab, handing the retrieved torch through the open space below the steel supports for the canvas.

David Jones lay face down, his right arm disappearing into the hatch in the floor. Unfortunately, the way Davie was lying his body covered all but one corner of the hatch, leaving just enough room for Pat to shine the torch down into the open gearbox, some 10 inches below the floor.

"Tank fuck for that. It doesn't look too bad. His hand is jammed, see what you think Harry."

"You OK for now Davie?" Harold asked as he changed places with Pat. A short inspection with the torch revealed that Davie's hand was trapped between the lower selector fork and the bearing support. Fortunately, there was no sign of blood.

"Looks like your hand is OK just trapped."

"Well, it doesn't feel that way from here. It's hurting like bloody blue murder." murmured the Welshman. It was obvious that the pain was almost more than Davie could bear.

"Hold on Davie. I just need to get my arm down beside yours and remove the screwdriver, then we can try and rock the truck back into gear. That should let us get your hand out. Ok?" Harold tried to sound convincing, he was worried about trying to get the truck back into gear. If they rocked it too far or too fast, then Davie's hand could well be pulled further into the gear cogs.

Harold stripped off his new donkey jacket. There wasn't much space so removing the extra bulky clothing would give him a better chance to reach down and retrieve the screwdriver. Seconds passed as he grunted and groaned with the effort of removing the trapped tool. What made it even harder was trying not to put any of his weight onto the injured Welshman. A difficult task in the limited space and proximity. Finally, after some minutes Harold managed to free the screwdriver, allowing the jammed selector to jump forward, relieving the pressure on Davie Jones crushed hand.

However, they still had to free his fingers from between the two gear shafts. It was fortunate that the gap between the two sets of cogs was only a little less than the thickness of Davie's short digits. When Rooster's foot had hit the starter button the gear-stick had been jammed in third. Luckily this was a relatively high gear. Had it been in first and the ignition on, the old truck engine would have started and continued to run; Davie's hand and arm would have been drawn into the gearbox. As it was the jolt from the starter had been enough to trap his four fingers. It was fortunate that the ignition had been off; in third gear, the truck engine simply lurched, as there wasn't enough power in the starter to turn over the heavy motor and move the truck.

Removing Davie's hand had to be the exact reverse of the manner it had been trapped. To get the correct cogs to turn, the truck would again have to be in third gear. If the clutch was depressed removing the engine load, then the rest of the gang should be able to push the truck backwards enough to reverse the sequence of events that trapped Davie's fingers.

Harold instructed Pat and the rest of the gang on what he wanted them to do; first, something should be placed an inch behind one of the front wheels, leaving the big tyres enough room to move back a little at a time, inching the gear train round until Davies' fingers were free of the mangle-like cogs.

In less than a minute the gang was set up for the delicate operation; Pat sat in the cab holding the heavy clutch pedal down to the floor while ensuring that the long straight gear-stick didn't jump out of third gear. Di Jones was stationed at the front wheel; his job was to move the block of wood back an inch at a time until his countryman's hand was freed. Wing-nut, Rooster, and the two riggers were placed at the front with their backs braced to push.

Harold lay beside Davie Jones, his own arm wrapped around the Welshman's wrist, ready to stop Davie pulling his hand free and doing more damage.

"Ok. Easy does it. Push it back against the block." The men obliged, pushing the truck back slowly till the tyre moved hard up against the wooden block. Harold had gently placed his index finger against the top cog. Being careful not to get his own digits trapped. The cog had moved round three teeth. Now Harold had a better idea of how far the truck would have to be moved.

Davie Jones wasn't doing so well. His hand had been swelling up, tightening the hold on his enlarged fingers. The pain was worse than anything he had ever felt before. It was so bad that beads of sweat were forming on his brow as he tried to hold back the urge to panic. Only the mild Scotsman's voice, encouraging him to keep still, stopped Davie Jones from trying to tear his hand from between the gears.

"Again." Shouted Harold. The gear turned another three teeth.

"More, move the stick back two inches dia." Again, the truck moved back.

"Hold it. You OK Davie? We're nearly there." Harold could feel Davis' fingers, now only the tips were caught. After another brief inspection, he shouted,

"Last one boys. Another two inches Di. Now push." Then Davie's hand was free. Harold carefully helped him withdraw the injured member from the hole. Fortunately, there was no blood. The skin hadn't been broken, but the flesh of Davie's hand was already going black from the mangling it had taken from the gears. Harold propped Davie up against the front of the truck, trying to make him as comfortable as possible. The winch-man's face was pale and ashen; any attempt to move the injured hand brought on waves of nausea.

Pat jumped up beside the two,

"How is he, Harry?" Asked the big ganger.

"don't know. Best get him to a hospital as soon as." Answered Harold already putting the top-plate back onto the gearbox. Di and Wing-nut had set about refitting the tarpaulin over the steel supports. Pat ordered the ropes and boxes be reloaded as quickly as possible.

Five minutes later Harold started the truck and headed for the local hospital some miles away. pushing the ancient Bedford as hard as it would go. It was thirteen miles to the nearest cottage hospital, on minor roads that rarely saw much traffic. Fortunately for Davie Jones, Harold knew just how to handle the old girl, and they arrived at the cottage hospital some forty-five minutes later. The boys in the back had shed their jackets, wrapping them around Davie in order to keep him as warm and comfortable as possible.

It was daylight by the time they lifted Davie Jones down from the back of the truck, placing him in a wheelchair, supplied by the stern-faced sister who had reluctantly come out to inspect Davie's mangled hand. There was no accident and emergency unit at the small hospital. The nearest one was in Chester some twenty miles away. The sister agreed to assess Davie and get an ambulance to take him the rest of the way. The thought of the injured Welshman travelling another twenty miles in the freezing open air was more than her stern heart would accept.

The sister insisted that Pat leave a statement on the accident, along with details on how to contact Davie's wife. The big ganger had been concerned for Davies health; any thoughts about informing his wife had gone out the window. Roosters carry-on had taken Pat's limited patience beyond any known limits. The final insult had been the cheeky scouser's rendition of the Irishman's mother's dubious virtues.

Once Rooster found a man's weakness he would exploit it ruthlessly without quarter. If he was pissed off, then he wouldn't be happy until everyone else was the same, niggling and insulting each member of the gang until all and sundry were in the same rattled state. It was the main reasons that Pat insisted the gang idiot ride in the cab. At least that way the rest of the men usually got to the site in fairly good humour. Now, for the first time in over a year, the wily Liverpudlian was banished to the back, forced to sit right next to the tailgate and instructed under pain of instant sacking to keep his mouth shut.

Chapter 8. Mark Thompson Bsc Eng.

It was nine thirty when the truck finally pulled into the erection site, a field in the middle of nowhere. The L2 pylon they were erecting stood minus its arms, right in the middle of a twenty-acre barley field. Either side of the base the gang had laboured to assemble the six arms that still had to be lifted up and secured to the steel tower.

The constant rain for the past few weeks had turned the site area into a quagmire. Now for the first time since the rain started the men could walk from the gate to the site hut without plummeting knee deep in mud. The first frost had crusted the soil just enough to support a man's weight without him sinking to his knees. Unfortunately, the warming sun would soon remove any advantage that the crisp frost had brought. By mid-day, they would again be struggling around in the sticky brown goo.

It would be days before the field drained enough for the truck to enter. Pat groaned as Harold stopped the vehicle just short of the wide gate. Over the hedge, he could see one of the company Landrovers bogged down to the axles, just fifteen feet into the field. The d6 number on the back door confirmed his worst fears.

"Fuck! If Davies accident isn't enough we've got this mad useless bastard to contend with. Get the boys over to the site and start setting up for the first lift. I'll try and keep this ejit out of your hair." Pat growled, swinging down from the cab. Making for the bogged land rover the big ganger shouted back to Wing-nut indicating that he should join him at the bogged vehicle. This was one time the lad's memory would be needed.

As the two of them approached the driver's side the door swung violently open, revealing an extremely tall and very heavyset man in his fifties. Without further preamble, the man jumped out and set on Pat.

"Where have you lot been. You should have been here an hour and a half ago." Pat was not getting a chance to reply.

"I want the first lift started in ten minutes and I'm not leaving here until all six lifts are finished." The engineer's face was red with frustration.

"Yes Sir, we can do dat." Pat answered, reverting to his most rural Irish accent. This particular engineer was well known for his obnoxious attitude. A graduate of Oxford he had never quite understood why the top jobs had always passed him by. In his own imagination, he should have been working on prestige projects, like the Forth Road Bridge, or the new motorways that were beginning to work their way across the country. Building pylons for what he believed to be a second-rate construction company wasn't his idea of success.

"But do you not think we should get diss Landrover outa-da mud first, Mr Thompson?" Continued Pat seemingly oblivious to the engineer's ferocious attempt to chastise him.

"No, I fucking well don't." Mark Thompson turned back on the pair who had remained standing by the back of the landrover. His right foot went down on the thin ice covering one of the water-filled ruts, left by the four tonner weeks before. He stumbled forward as his leg just kept going down landing prostrate on the edge of the rut. His right-side soaking-wet from foot to groin. For a few seconds, he just lay there stunned and enraged by the freezing muddy water as it worked its way into his right Wellington boot.

Both Pat and Wing-nut turned away doing their best not to laugh at the ludicrous antics of the furious engineer. The big Irishman unceremoniously pushed Wing-nut behind the Landrover not wanting the boy to suffer the indignities, he himself was about to receive.

Turning back, he asked in his thickest Irish accent,

"Would you be alright Mr Thompson?" Mark Thompson froze. He couldn't believe what he had just heard. Attempting to get up, his right hand went through the ice dumping his face back down on the thawing mud.

"Help me up you fucking idiot." Roared the engineer holding his now soaking arm above the cracked ice. Pat moved forward to help the struggling man.

"Sure sir, I'll do dat. What do you want me to do sir?" Pat was bending over beside Mark Thompson's head with his best poker face on.

"Just help me get up." Pat took hold of Mark Thompson's left arm and began to assist him gently pushing forward at the same time. What happened next resembled a Laurel and Hardy comedy sketch. Thompson's right boot had stuck fast in the thick goo-like clay at the bottom of the rut. As Pat lifted him, an attempt to pull his left foot up under his centre of gravity failed, as the sole of his left Wellington slipped on the thawing mud.

Mark Thompson's own weight did the rest; all Pat had to do was hold his left arm up half a second longer than he should have, creating a moving pivot for the man's oversized body. The net result was that the engineer found himself on his side in the rut, almost totally immersed in the dirty brown water.

Pat decided that this farce had gone far enough. Now he had a chance to get rid of the incompetent superior. Surely he would go back to his digs for a change of clothes. Shouting for assistance from Wing-nut, they quickly struggled to get the drenched engineer free, leaving his right Wellington boot stuck in the mud.

Thompson leaned against the side of the Landrover, his dripping right foot held four inches above the rapidly thawing soil. dirty water streamed down his face, disappearing under the neck of his sodden shirt. Pat almost felt sorry for the bedraggled engineer.

"You'll be wanting the Landrover pulled out of the field Sir, will you not?" Pat asked, maintaining his thick Mick act. Wing-nut retrieved the lost Wellington and held it out to the drenched engineer symbolically pouring the last drops of dirty water from the boot, right in front of Mark Thompson's face.

The engineer reached out and snatched the boot from the boy's hand, glaring menacingly at the innocent looking pair.

"Yes, we will pull the fucking Landrover out of the fucking mud. Then, we will get on with building this fucking pylon. do you understand me you; you fucking Irish moron." The words had been deliberate and forceful; designed to cause serious insult to Pat and had been paced out in order to emphasise each instruction. No attempt had been made to hide his contempt for the Irishman or his race.

The big foreman knew this was shaping up to be one bastard of a day. First Rooster's tomfoolery and then Davie's accident. Now being a man down with this arrogant fool standing over them, he had no doubt that there was more to follow. This particular engineer was well known for his stupidity. On the odd occasions that Pat met any of the other ganger's Mark Thompson's name was sure to be mentioned.

So far Pat had managed to keep his own foul temper in check. Leaving the angry engineer propped up against the side of the company Landrover he and Wing-nut retrieved a tow chain from the back of the truck and secured it to the rear of the bogged Jeep. Pat then jumped into the truck and reversed the heavy vehicle in through the gate. Stopping before the rear wheels entered the deep puddle that spread between the wooden gateposts.

Wing-nut silently dragged the other end of the chain to the truck and dropped the thick draw-bar pin into the enlarged link at the end of the chain. Then moved into the driving seat of the Landrover; before joining the squad the lad had never learned to drive. At home most folk never went any further than Penzance, and then only on the bus.

One of his first lessons had been pulling the four tonner out of a ditch with one of the heavy county tractors. Pat had started the tractor telling him to hold down the clutch pedal. Then the Irishman knocked the tractor into a low gear, jumped clear and then mounted the disabled truck. All Gerald had to do was lift his foot off the clutch and steer the slow-moving tractor across the field. Now after numerous boggings during the last year, the lad had become proficient in removing bogged vehicles from a variety of disabling situations, handling the big four-wheel drive tractor with ease.

The County was equipped with a large spade-like blade, which when lowered would anchor the tractor against the pull of the main winch-gear. When lifting, the vehicle would be placed about one hundred yards away from the side of the pylon. The blade was then lowered and driven forward into the ground. A control rope was run across from a pulley under the pylon base, looped through a block anchored to the now embedded spade, then back towards the tower. It was fixed to the hook at the end of the main lift rope, which dangled from a block secured to a small Derek, attached to the top of the tower.

Between Davie and Di Jones, the pair would hoist the lift up the side of the pylon co-coordinating both winches in a manner that allowed the payload to travel upwards only inches from the metal framework.

Now with Davie injured Pat and Harold were the only other men experienced enough to operate the control lift. Harold couldn't do it, his job was aloft, securing the lift once it had been hoisted up into place. That meant that Pat would have to do it himself.

As foreman, the big Irishman normally stood back using a form of hand-signals to coordinate the lift with Davie and Di. Signals had to be used as the noise from the winch-engine drowned out all voice communications. One advantage of keeping Wing-nut close to him was the lad had a good knowledge of how the gang worked. The only jobs he wasn't allowed to do were up the pylon. Twice the Irishman had allowed him to try climbing, and twice the lad had to be helped down petrified. Some people just can't work aloft.

Pat and Wing-nut stowed the heavy chain in the side-locker of the truck and then made their way back to the Landrover now parked on the verge outside the gate. Mark Thompson had thrown open the back door of the vehicle and was rummaging through a large suitcase. Without further ado he stripped off his wet clothes and started to dry himself down with a large red bath towel, glaring at the pair every time their eyes met.

This was bad news. Without a doubt, the engineer intended to stay on site. Now Pats worst fears would become fact. Scowling; he and Wing-nut left the almost naked engineer and headed across the field on foot.

The late October sun was beginning to thaw the night's frost, making the top layer of soil act like glue caking their boots with copious quantities of sticky brown mud. As they made their way across the open field, Harold and Di Jones started the engine on the first County Tractor. Harold had encouraged them to warm up the engines before putting the heavy winch gear into action. As a result, there had been far fewer accidents from cold stressed machinery compared to other gangs in the company.

With little more than a nod, Pat indicated that Wing-nut should make directly for the other County and warm it up.

Davie and Di habitually worked the rig for fifteen minutes or so, carefully straining the ropes and pulleys. Cold and frozen ropes became hard and were more likely to break under strain. Working the gear generally squeezed the water out of them in much the same manner as wringing out wet clothes.

This morning after three weeks of rain and little use it would be even more important to work the gear. Hemp ropes had a tendency to rot when they were left wet. The first job after warm-up should be a full inspection of both the ropes and tackle.

Pat finally made it to the base of the pylon hampered by the balls of sticky mud that had attached to his Wellington boots. The thought of having Mark Thompson on his back all day wasn't one to incite a favourable mood. They would have to be even more careful than normal.

Pat spotted Tom, the senior rigger, pulling tackle from the four-wheel trailer they used as a store. The short thick set Geordie was from Sunderland, not strictly a true Geordie, but close enough for the rest of Britain. Both the riggers were extremely good at their jobs and like Harold, very conscientious about the care of their equipment.

Chapter 9. Tom.

On their way across the site, the senior rigger had split off from the rest and made for the second County. As an anchor for the control rope, this pulley block carried more strain than any other single part of the rig. If it failed or the County slipped, the results could be catastrophic. Tons of steel crashing into the main structure would result in them having to tear the whole damned thing down and start again.

On two separate occasions over his ten years as a rigger, he had seen this happen. Both times with fatal consequences. The first had been in Rhodesia. The second several years later in India. Both incidents had claimed the lives of close friends.

Leaving the spade buried in the ground had its risks. With all the rain, water would find its way down into the clay, softening it around the huge steel spade. In extreme circumstances it might be possible for the subsoil above the blade to fail, allowing the whole assembly to be pulled out of the ground. If that happened all that would hold the rig in place would be the tractors massive weight. On dry soil, this would not be a problem. Here it would be like pulling a sitting dog across the ice with a string leash.

Sheltered by the overhanging blade, the pool of clear water that had accumulated under the steel spade bore only the thinnest coating of ice. Tom retrieved a small spade from the Counties toolbox and made a few exploratory stabs through the water into the bottom of the puddle. The main body of the clay was still hard, so far suffering only minimal softening. The senior rigger had little doubt that the soil in front of the spade would easily survive three lifts. Although when it came to moving the County round to the other side he had his doubts.

Next, he moved to the heavy anchor post that rose two feet above the back of the blade. Placed centrally between the two support arms, the post was designed to maximise the effect of the spade and the tractor's weight. Once the massive blade had been dozed into the clay, the hydraulics lifted the front of the tractor off the topsoil adding most of the heavy machine's weight to the force, holding the spade into the ground.

The post was solid steel; about six inches square with an inch thick plate welded vertically down the front. The welded plate had a number of one and a half inch holes drilled at four-inch intervals, allowing the riggers to set their pulleys at different heights above ground level increasing or decreasing the effort required to overcome the tractor's holding force.

A third link ran from a clevis pin on top of the post to the heavy casting just below the massive radiator on the tractor chassis, ensuring that the anchor always maintained a particular stance. If required the connecting link could be shortened, allowing the head of the post to be set back or forward, depending on the situation.

Tom preferred to set the post halfway between the horizontal and the maximum angle that the control rope would make with the ground equalising the forces on the post and pulley mount.

As usual, the steel post and the big shackle that held the pulley block were in good shape. Not so the metal pulley. Close inspection showed that the pulley-wheel was lying to one side, a definite indication that the bush was wearing unevenly, or was in danger of imminent collapse. The block should be replaced before the lift began. Failure to do so could mean the pulley seizing inside the block and causing the rope to jam.

Unfortunately, Tom had a feeling that this was the only pulley heavy enough to carry this particular weight. Pat was not going to be happy about this. Changing the block could mean pulling hundreds of yards of rope out through the block contaminating the wet hemp with brown sticky mud.

A quick glance told him that Matt the other rigger was steadily climbing the near leg of the tower. Younger and more agile than Tom he would check the pulleys and tackle at the top of the pylon. Shading his eyes against the glare of the sun, Tom could see the dark shadow of a grease gun looped through the younger man's belt. Matt always greased the bushes whenever he went aloft.

Retrieving a gun from the County toolbox Tom pumped copious quantities of the dark sticky grease through the ailing bush. If they could get the first lift out of it at least they would achieve something. A quick check of the pins and bushes on the spade revealed nothing else of any interest.

Tom made his way back to the pylon area where walking boards had been laid out to help the men get around the site. It had been the only way the gang had managed to work during the preceding three weeks. It was normal practice to build the arms on the ground and then when all six had been assembled, lift them up into place, securing them to the main tower. As usual, the arms had been supported on piles of second-hand railway sleepers keeping them off the ground while still allowing the men to work on all the joints.

The arms consisted of relatively small four-sided pyramids, the width of the main tower at the thick end whittling down to a point at a distance, approximately three times the thickness of the main tower. The length varied depending on the requirements of each particular pylon. As this one was in the middle of a long straight section some four miles long, the arms on both sides were exactly the same length, allowing for only a single string of insulators on each wire-pair.

Tom made straight for the mobile store. Using the small ladder that had been welded to the frame just under the door to climb the four or so feet into the van, scraping the accumulated mud from his boots on the last rung. After some five minutes digging around in the dark piles of pulley blocks, Tom finally found what he had been looking for. It was a broken block similar to the one on the anchor County.

The securing ring had been bent out of shape when Rooster had dropped the blade of the County onto it some months before. The pulley pin and bush on this one were in good condition, only the securing ring was bent out of shape. There should be enough parts between the two blocks to make one good one. Harold could probably split the block without having to remove the rope and replace the faulty pulley in less than an hour if Pat would let them.

Tom decided it would be better to get everything ready, and then if they were given the go-ahead, time would be saved stripping the donor block. A quick look in the direction of the gate told him things weren't going well for Pat. The engineer was standing against the Landrover giving the big Irishman a piece of his mind. Even across the field, his angry voice was unmistakable. So much for things getting better as the day went on.

A morbid 'I've been here before." feeling crept up out of the depths of Tom's mind. This day had all the trappings of that horrible day in Africa. There too, one of the men had been injured in a stupid accident on the way to work. After that thing's had gone from bad to worse. The injured man had been the chief rigger, which meant that he would have to do the senior job while he was absent.

The ganger on that job had been a foul-tempered Belgian midget called Hans. The bastard had been selling new gear off to the local farmers, leaving them with ropes that were worn and frayed, and blocks that were ready to break. The rest of the machinery was breaking down constantly from lack of maintenance. Sooner or later something had to give.

He'd had a fight with Hans that morning over the state of the top pulley. Like this one, the bush in the centre was breaking up. Tom had taken the initiative when his normally placid senior wasn't there. He finally had to give in to the devious European, when the bastard had pushed the barrel of a revolver up his nose. Tom had given in instantly. They were miles away from the nearest settlement. Being forced to walk through the bush on his own wasn't a risk Tom had been prepared to take.

Pat had a foul temper every bit as bad as Hans. However, there the similarities ended. The big Irishman had never been known to compromise safety for a few quid or even allow himself to be bullied into dangerous situations. Today with this particular engineer Tom knew that Pat's metal was going to be tested to the limit.

Chapter 10. Matt.

From his vantage point at the top of the main tower, Matt could see for miles across the Cheshire countryside. To the east several miles away he could clearly see a large freighter slowly making her way up the Manchester shipping canal towards the Irish sea. The ship reminded him of his father.

"His Father!" The last time he had seen him was fourteen years ago. The bastard had told his mum he was just going down the pub for a pint. The silly old girl was still waiting for him to come home. Weeks later they had been told he had signed up on a freighter and was on his way to Hong Kong. The old bastard had never settled down after the war. Five years on liberty ships ploughing back and forth across the Atlantic had instilled a love of the sea far greater than the pull of his family. Civy street had been more than he could take.

Even working on the dock hadn't brought him any satisfaction. Each time he threw a hawser from bollard, a part of him sailed down the Thames along with the departing ship. Matt bore little animosity for his father. Several years after he had sailed into the sunset, his mother told him she had been waiting for it to happen for years.

"Always loved the sea, he did. One of these days he'll walk back in that door as if nothing had happened." She had told him. So far it hadn't occurred. Now Matt had a wife and two young children of his own. It had always puzzled him that his mother had never sought a divorce. At 45 she was still a fairly young woman and going by the talk in the local pub there were any number of potential suitors lining up to get close to her. She had steadfastly stuck to her guns, turning each down flat. Stating simply that,

"Her Matt would be home from the sea soon and he wouldn't like it."

Matt quivered at the thought of leaving his own wife and young children alone to fend for themselves. Reluctantly he forced his thoughts back to the task at hand. Hooking his safety harness around the crossbeam, he swung easily out to where the block was anchored to the small derek. Everything was in order. A good five pumps of grease would ensure that they wouldn't have any problems with these blocks.

The late October sunshine was beginning to melt the remaining frost generating streaming wisps of water vapour that danced upward in the still air. Even the thick hemp rope was beginning to produce similar streamers as the outer surface of the fibre bundles soaked up the energy from the weak morning sun. The rope looked fine, wet through, but there were no obvious kinks or frayed sections within view. Time to get back down. The sound of raised voices drifted up from the field gate. Apparently, the engineer was having a go at Pat and Wing-nut.

Below Tom was climbing into the store. Matt wondered what was up, something must be either broken or about to break. The senior rigger wasn't one for letting things develop.

Harold and di Jones were both at the main winch engine, doing the daily checks before starting the big eight-cylinder Ford engine. This one had the heavier winch and an even larger blade than its counterpart. The makers suggested that it was capable of pulling itself up a near vertical cliff, using only the auxiliary winch gear. God knows what it could do using the full power of the main winch.

He could hear the big engine turning over, forcing puff after puff of blue-white smoke from the once vertical exhaust. Harold held the starter engaged for perhaps thirty seconds before releasing the switch. He would heat the engine for another half minute before trying again.

Matt started down watching the dissolving clouds from the tractor exhaust float slowly toward the east near the base of the structure well below his feet. The step bolts were placed three feet apart on two sides of the five-inch angle iron that made up the outside corner of the structure. The two sides were staggered so that each step was only eighteen inches or the equivalent of two normal stairs apart. Six-inch long bolts, double bolted through the upright angle formed the step pegs. Once you got the feel of the extended stride it was surprising how quickly one could ascend the pylon, even laden down with coils of heavy rope or bags of nuts and bolts.

After a few months, the climbing became automatic, not effortless, but the mind seemed to switch off, allowing time out for thoughts to wander. Matt's favourite was his seven-month-old daughter Lisa, barely able to crawl, she would lie on her stomach and make swimming motions with her arms and legs while chuckling and goo-ing happily at Martin or herself.

It was surprising how protective Martin her two-year-old brother was. He would spend time playing with his little sister, patiently watching her wriggle closer to the edge of the bed. When she was in danger of falling over the edge, the toddler would scold her then drag her back from the brink. Turning her over onto her back, Lisa would giggle and squirm until she again managed to turn herself over. Then the whole game would be repeated.

Matt wondered at his son, the child was fast losing his toddler wobble in favour of the tiny little man look. Even his vocabulary was improving by the day. Most evenings when he returned home to the caravan site in Easter Mingthorpe. Gwen would have folded down the table between the two divan beds and slipped it in under the foam mattresses. Adding the back cushions to the table top turned the whole front of the caravan into one big bed. Harold had built a fold-away wooden fence for Gwen some months before, allowing her to pen both children on the big bed. It was a very practical arrangement that allowed Matt's young wife to get on with her chores without the children being under her feet.

Most days both children would fall asleep around four in the afternoon, tired out after playing all day. Martin would cuddle up beside Lisa and both would fall asleep. Recently the toddler had been waking up ten minutes or so before he arrived. The child seemed to know when his dad was approaching, bouncing up and down excitedly on the thick foam mattresses while using the wooden fence as support.

Matt's first duty on entering the van, after shedding his bulky work clothes, was a trip to the pen, hoisting Martin up over the wooden fence, the toddler would hug him as tightly as the child could, babbling excitedly, trying to tell his dad about the events of the day. Martins vocabulary was very limited at two. Fortunately, Gwen would interpret, filling in the gaps that exuberance and incomplete language invariably left.

His thought turned to Harold. Earlier, while they had been waiting for Pat to finish writing out the accident report at the cottage hospital, the canny Scotsman had told them that Mavis was finally pregnant. Everyone with the exception of the sin-died Rooster had congratulated him, patting him on the back and vigorously shaking his hand.

Gwen and Mavis were close friends, as were most of the wives. Where possible they all tried to get the vans parked in the same facility. This time there hadn't been enough room on either site for them all. So Pat and Harold had elected to take the farthest away park. Well, it was good sense. Both men drove the four tunner. If one of them wasn't fit then the other would still be able to get the rest of the gang to work.

Below, Harold was turning over the winch engine again, this time the she fired intermittently for several seconds before returning to the flat, Wa-Wa! This was her normal behaviour at low temperatures. Sometimes if it was really cold Harold would light an oily rag and hold it in front of the huge air intake. Allowing the engine to suck in warm air.

Harold maintained that the engine required new injectors. Unfortunately, company policy meant that unless equipment failed completely it stayed on site. The fitters were encouraged to get things working again, not to take them out of commission. The downside of this attitude was that on most of the sites, little real maintenance took place.

The fitters were constantly harassed chasing from site to site patching things together. Most of the time they were sent to a breakdown with only the sketchiest of information. They would arrive to find out that the information the clerk had given them was often nothing to do with the site they were visiting. However, because of the state of the equipment and the lack of regular maintenance the gangers usually insisted that some piece of equipment or another required fixing immediately, further holding up the emergency repair.

Thanks to Harold, when a fitter was required on site Pat would always be armed with concise notes. The Irishman always insisted the clerk read the notes back to him before allowing the overworked individual to end the call. Now when a fitter was told he was going to Pat's site, they all insisted on reading the dictated notes before leaving. The result was that when they did have to visit; their vans usually contained parts and equipment required for the job.

There was an even more positive side to this relationship. Tom and Harold habitually kept a record of the state of the machinery on the site. When something was wearing or was in danger of failing, the first fitter to come to the site would be given an order and a copy of the notes to be passed back to the head fitter on returning to the workshops. As a result, most of the mobile plant on Pat's site was better maintained than any other squad in the company. The mobile fitters had even started calling in unannounced if they were in the area. Not to do any work but in case Pat or Harold required anything next time they passed anywhere near.

The knock-on effect was that Mike O'mahony, the head fitter had dedicated a corner of the workshop to items that were needed by Pat's gang. Any time one of his men would be going in their direction, they would be asked to check the corner first or even check it before asking. So far the system had worked out well. Costs related to this particular squad had been consistently lower than the other erection gangs. Mike had even started touring the sites at the end of the month, under the guise of doing safety checks. As a result, he had a better picture of which squads required the most looking after. It was his subtle attempt to institute a similar arrangement with the other gangers. So far the results had been mixed.

Matt stepped off the concrete foundation and jumped lightly onto the walking boards that ran right around the pylon base. The County had finally fired up and was now running at a fast idle, billowing a streaming cloud of dark smoke. Harold never allowed the equipment to tick-over when cold, fearing that thick oil wouldn't flow through the engine as easily as warm oil, so for two minutes or so he would run the engine at about half throttle, then progressively reduce the setting as the engine warmed up.

Normally Davie and Di would test the rig while she was warming up. Working the winches and hydraulics. It wouldn't do for the winch to pack in halfway through a lift just because a brake band had rusted onto the drum. This morning that was a distinct possibility. Happy that they had successfully started the main engine, Harold jumped up onto the control platform beside Di. This morning he would assist the Welshman with running up the rig.

Matt moved along the walking boards to the anchor point directly under the pylon. Here a large H-beam had been sunk into the ground. On top of this five-foot high post, an arrangement of slings and pulleys directed the winch ropes from the

County upwards and outwards from the pylon, allowing the big tractor to sit in one place during the entire erection of the tower.

Tensioned wire slings anchored the pulleys to the base of each pylon leg, holding the block down against the lifting force of the main gear. Again, Matt checked the pulleys and blocks for any obvious signs of wear or breakage, then as usual applied a suitable quantity of grease.

Sometimes a change in the weather required that the turnbuckles in each of the four anchor cables be adjusted slackening or tightening to compensate for the change in temperature. Four days ago, when they had finished constructing the last leg, Harold had slackened the slings. There was no reason to keep them under tension until the main lifts began. Now with the first frost, the heavy wire slings had contracted, building the tension in the ropes. A rattle with his spike indicated that the slings had contracted just enough to hold them taut. They would do for now; later on, as the day got warmer he would have to tighten each up a few turns.

Happy that there were no problems with the tackle Matt joined Tom at the mobile store.

"What's up Tom?" he asked spotting the partly damaged block. Now partially disassembled.

"Pulley in the anchor block is tipping over. I think the bush is breaking up. This is the only other block with that rating." Matt leaned over,

"That's the one Rooster fucked with the blade." Tom nodded,

"We need to change it, but with that nutter on site. I don't Know. Here, hold the block while I slacken the bolts."

Chapter 11. The Winch.

Mounting his side of the control platform, Harold took his place at the auxiliary winch control position. The main console formed a "T" shape with the two operators separated by a deep eighteen-inch wide housing. Numerous slot's had been cut in the upper surface, allowing ancillary control levers to protrude through. Unfortunately, the manufacturers of this particular winch had not provided dual controls on each side, hence the requirement for two operators.

Harold gave Di the thumbs up signal. Indicating to the Welshman that he could proceed with the winch test. The Welshman nodded and pulled back the long clutch lever, disengaging the power take-off clutch. The solid steel bar stood a full three feet tall, and it needed to be. The drive for the PTO was expected to stand up to anything they threw at it. Even with the thirty to one ratio built into the lever, it still required a solid heave to operate. In contrast, the drive selector was a stubby little lever only three inches long, which protruded from the centre console just about knee height, right next to his left leg. Once the Clutch lever had been fully pulled back it only took a fingertip to drop the lever into gear.

Both Harold and Di checked that all the winch controls were either in neutral or locked off. Engaging the clutch while a winch was engaged could have dire consequences for the tackle. Di had seen blocks ripped from the pylon top just because the winch-man hadn't checked properly when starting the drive. Some liked to force the lever forward, banging the drive in quickly. Both Davie and Di preferred to work the clutch in slowly, ensuring that the drive into the gearbox took up smoothly without undue stress. That way if the drive train had seized pressure on the components they could be released before stalling the massive engine or damaging the gearbox.

Di slowly inched the big lever forward listening intently for the change of engine note that indicated a load was being applied to the PTO. Normally the lever would travel easily to the vertical before any real force was required. As the stout metal bar was forced beyond this point, the engine began to slow, increasing both the depth and volume of the sound. As always it was accompanied by a plume of dark fumes rushing from the engine exhaust. Apparently indicating the engines displeasure at having a load applied to its output.

An unfamiliar clanking sound reminiscent of a rotating component banging hard off a stationary object sounded above the roar of the engine. Di immediately pulled back allowing the drive to disengage. Stopping the drive with a sudden and loud series of bangs. The Welshman looked across at Harold who had already pulled the strangler, killing the big diesel.

Suddenly silence reigned around the winch. As soon as the engine stopped Harold pulled the cover from the PTO housing which lay at the bottom of the central console between the two operators stations.

Each operator was protected from the huge winch drum by a metal casing that held the control lever for their respective winch. Behind each a travelling pulley fed the rope on or off the drum neatly from side to side, ensuring that the ropes were wound evenly across the full width.

The rope then ran back under the operator and was guided around two fixed pulleys, which sent it upwards under the central housing before another set of wheels finally directed them downwards over the transfer gearbox and out through the exit ports low down between the massive winding drums.

The whole arrangement had been mounted on the two stout arms that formed the blade supports. Sitting close behind the six-foot diameter rear wheels the heavy unit had been designed to increase the effective weight transfer to the spade when pulling. A secondary arrangement of hydraulic rams under the winch allowed the operator to raise or lower the unit depending on the ground conditions and the force required.

The cover removed, Harold spotted the problem. One of the spikes they used when bolting the angle irons together had fallen through the upper casing and lodged in the yoke of the rear universal joint. The spanner stopped the spike from falling straight through. When the shaft was turned, the fourteen-inch long spike had jammed against one of the hydraulic rams. The force of the massive engine had bent the tapering spike like a piece of soft wire wrapping the spike around the rotating shaft. The centripetal force pushed the bent metal outwards hitting the ram on either side as the assembly rotated.

Both ram casings showed bright silver scars where the metal spike had impacted. Had the drive not been stopped, the metal cylinders could have been severely damaged. Fortunately, the metal spike had only rotated about five time's, barely long enough for the shaft to reach anything like its full rotational velocity. Di's quick reactions had averted a minor disaster.

Harold reached in and tried to free the twisted spike from the yoke of the universal joint. The spike was slack and could easily be moved, but due to the way the metal had been wrapped around the shaft, it was impossible to remove inside the confines of the winch gear. Being based on a modified agricultural machine the drive shaft was like one found on any tractor. Consisting of two quick fit ends that slid over a splined shaft at either end. Two universal joints allowed the shaft to operate up to 45 degrees from true. The centre part of the shaft was telescopic, allowing for extension or contraction depending on what height the operator chose to set the unit.

Being an adaptation and not a purpose-built system had its advantages. The shaft could easily be detached and pulled back to just around three-quarters of its working length. The other end could then be disconnected from the drive shaft on the tractor back end, allowing the assembly to be rotated into a near vertical position. Then it could easily be pulled out through the cowling.

With Di's help, Harold disconnected the shaft and hauled it out onto the platform. At first glance, the damage had been limited to the strikes on the support ram casings. Now that he had the assembly out in full daylight it was obvious that the delicate needle bearings that allowed the shaft to work at an angle had been severely damaged. Not really a big deal, Harold knew he could change both couplings in around half an hour. The real problem was they didn't have any spares on site. This was one of those rare occasions when they would be forced to call out a fitter.

Pat trudged up to the county easily pulling himself up onto the platform.

"Fuck! Of all the days for this to happen. How bad is it Harry?"

"Spicer bearings are smashed on the gearbox end."

"Where the fuck did that spike come from?"

"Must be the one Rooster lost the other week. Stupid bastard launched it from up top." Pat kicked the casing.

"What's the odds that fucking idiot has dropped a spanner in the works again." Neither Harry nor Di answered Pat was angry enough without them making fun of his unconscious pun.

Pat looked across the field towards the gate. Mike Thompson still hadn't finished re-dressing himself. Scowling Pat turned back to Harold,

"See if you can strip the coupling down, then both of you give Tom and Matt a hand to change the block on the anchor. Harry give me a list of the parts you need for the shaft."

"Is Tom trying to get the pulley from the block Rooster busted a few months ago." Pat nodded.

"It's been modified, someone has bored out the bush and put a larger one in. If he tries to change them over, the new one won't fit on the block." Pat took a deep breath.

"Bastard. You better list the size of block we need. The fitter can bring one down with the coupling. Di go and tell Tom not to bother."

Pat handed Harold his notebook as the Welshman jumped lightly down from the winch and made his way towards the mobile store. Moments later the other two followed heading for the damaged block on the other County. Where a quick inspection revealed the type and specification of the block.

drawing his finger across his throat, Harold indicated that Wing-nut shut the engine down on the second machine. It would be well into the morning before they would be ready for the first lift.

Chapter 12. Mike O'mahony.

The battered Morris 1000 van was in fact only two years old. Most of the fitters tended to treat the vehicle like it was going around the track at Silverstone. He already had to replace the diff after one of the ganger's insisted that a fitter try and pull a twelve-ton winch tractor out of a ditch. Mike marvelled at the little vehicle, it's narrow fifteen-inch wheels could take the driver through places that the newer Mini-vans couldn't go.

Had he been allowed to participate in the decision, Mike would have done his best to prevent the ordering of the newer Minivans. The old Morris's had proved their worth, while the Mini's were small and the engines hard to work on. There was little room around the transverse engine for a mechanic to work. The front wheel drive while giving excellent handling on the road, fell down when they tried to cross soft ground with a load on. The Morris had a tendency to cut through the soft soil finding dryer earth beneath, having fifteen-inch wheels instead of ten inch, allowed the van to sink in without grounding. With a load on the buggers would go just about anywhere.

However, he had to admit the fitters loved the new vans. They were fast and extremely agile. Personally, he suspected that someone in the buying department had received a fat bonus for the deal. Now the Lone Morris Van was his to do with as he pleased, all the rest had been sold on as part of the package. Even then Mike had to dig in his heels, insisting that they needed at least one larger van. Not all the small plant could be fitted inside the Mini's. Especially if the fitter had his tools and equipment packed in too.

There were four sites working on the string passing through Cheshire. Two digging, one foundation, and Pat's erection squad. The wire stringers weren't due to start for another four months, Once the last leg was started. All except Pat's squad had been laid off because of the rain. You can't dig holes in the ground when they fill up with water as quickly as you dig them. Nor was the foundation gang able to pour concrete in the extremely wet weather. Pat's men had escaped the layoff, only because they could spend their time assembling the arms ready for lifting.

There was a good side to things. Mike's own men had been able to catch up on some much-needed maintenance. Most of the small mobile plant had been recalled to the workshop before the men had been laid off. Two fitters and three apprentices had been locked in the workshop for the last three weeks. Now finally they were beginning to see the light at the end of the tunnel.

Earlier in the month Pat had called in and ordered some oil, grease and filters for the servicing of both the winch engines and the four-ton Bedford truck. There were also slings and chains that had been refurbished and were ready for return to the site.

The previous night Mike had filled the Morris van to the brim with the assortment of parts and equipment that were overdue for delivery to Pat's site. It would be a four-hour drive across country, so he deemed it prudent to leave the workshop around 6 am. Expecting to arrive around ten.

Yesterday Mike Simpson the regional manager had called into the workshops. Mike was one of the few decent managers in the company. In his early sixties, any ambitions of climbing higher up the promotional ladder had long since been put out to pasture. Now the fat balding little man was more interested in making sure that everything worked out as planned.

Mike Simpson had a knack for predicting job times, almost down to the hour. Somehow, neither wind nor weather seemed to affect his calculations. In fact, most times, the job would be finished a day or two prior to Mike's predicted date. When questioned about the apparent error Mike just smiled and gave a little shrug of the shoulders. What the younger men forgot was that two days in a five-year project was such a small percentage it hardly mattered.

The company had just won the contract for a new string that would run from Hastings up towards London and then up through the Midlands, connecting some of the remaining gaps in what was fast becoming known as the National Grid. The design was impressive, the implications phenomenal. For the first time in England's history, Electrical power would be available twenty-four hours a day, 365 days of the year. If for some reason, there was a failure in one regional power station the grid would compensate by routing power from other areas. In essence, the countries supply would be consistent, whatever the geographical region.

New gangs would be required to build the new string. Fortunately, the diggers and foundation squads would be finished their current assignments just about the time when they would be required to start the new line. That meant only one new erection gang would be added to the existing workforce.

The two men had sat in conference most of the day, working out the logistics of getting the new project up and running. Finally, around three thirty they had got down to who would run the new erection squad. Strictly speaking, Mike O'mahony didn't have anything to do with organising the who's who of the labour force. But both men had started out in the same squad nearly forty years earlier. Throughout the years Mike Simpson had come to rely on his third-generation Irish friends wisdom. Mike knew his equipment, his men, and which squads could be trusted to get the job done.

One name kept cropping up. Harold. The mild-mannered Scotsman seemed to be just right for the job. He knew plant; he was a climber, and most of all he could inspire men. The only fly in the ointment was his climbing partner. In the air, they were legendary. On the ground, well that was a different story. One thing both men were sure of the red-haired scouser who complimented Harold when climbing would not be part of the same squad.

Both men failed to understand, why such a capable man had consistently refused to take up the responsibility. The men weren't that well paid. The extra money that the foreman's job would bring could make a big difference to their family's financial stability. during their conversation, Mike O'mahony indicated that he was planning to send one of the fitters over to service both winch engines and the four-ton Bedford used by Pat's squad. Mike Simpson, knowing that the squad shouldn't be attempting the final lifts for a few days, suggested that his old friend, take a day out and drive over to Cheshire, himself. While he was there, if by chance Harold was assisting him with the servicing then Mike might broach the subject of promotion, possibly mentioning the benefits that the increased money could bring.

Mike was pleased with his boss's suggestion. Being cooped up in the office and adjoining workshops was beginning to wear on him. The thought of a nice drive across country was appealing. Pat and his men were good crack. A day with them would certainly raise his spirits.

Chapter 13. The standoff

Pat trudged back towards the gate, his mood darkening with each muddy step. If the heater in the D6 Landrover performed like the one in the four-toner. Thompson would be in there for most of the morning. It was perhaps fortunate that the arrogant bastard only had one set of Wellington boots with him. There were a couple of spare pairs in the back of the four-toner, but the wily Irishman wasn't about to let him know that. The longer they could keep him off the site the better.

As Pat trudged through the large puddle at the gate the familiar sound of a Morris van decelerating turned his attention along the road away from the Landrover.

"Thank fuck for that," Pat whispered to himself. The sight of Mike O'mahony behind the wheel raised his spirits considerably, inserting a spring in the big man's step for the first time that morning. Now at least he would have a chance of getting things back on track. Mike's opinions of Thompson were well known in the company. Neither man had any time for the other. In an attempt to rid himself of the load on each Wellington, Pat stamped his way across the single tarmac road.

Mike had pulled the Morris up onto the verge opposite the open gate. Smiling at the big Irishman Mike opened the van door. Over the years they had developed a good solid friendship. Mike was, in fact, Pat's first daughter's godfather.

After the usual exchange of greetings, Mike nodded towards the parked Landrover and asked.

"What's that pillock doing here? Mike Simpson told me you won't be ready to lift for another few days." Frowning, Pat answered.

"The bastards out for brownie points wants all six lifts done today." Then continued, brightening.

"You should have been here half an hour ago. The bastard nearly drowned in one of the ruts. Soaked from head to foot he was."

"Does he know." Mikes face twisted forming a wicked smile extending almost from ear to ear. Which faded as he noticed the notebook in Pat's hand.

"What's up?" He asked nodding toward the erection site across the field.

"The universal joints on the PTO shaft collapsed when Harry and Di tried to run her up this morning. Some stupid fucker dropped a spike down through one of the openings in the casing. Of all the places, it lodged its self in the yoke behind the hardy-spicer. Its wrapped around the shaft like a python around a pig. Harry's trying to get it off. You wouldn't happen to carry a spare in the back of this oversized toy box. Would you?" Pat looked hopefully at his friend.

Mike closed one eye and thought deeply for several seconds. Old habits die-hard and like most of the fitters, the head mechanic habitually carried a selection of items that were liable to break unexpectedly. Hardy Spicer couplings for PTO shafts fell into that category. Lack of grease could destroy a universal joint in a matter of hours.

"Is it a three inch or a four-inch?" Mike asked dreamily, meticulously going through the contents of the van in his mind.

"A four-inch." Pat knew Mike would know the contents of the van right down to the last copper washer. He was the same in the workshop. Every item in every bin location could be called up using the same methodical technique. Much to the consternation of the not too energetic store-men.

"I should have. Let's have a look." Swinging out of the van Mike led Pat to the back.

"Fuck me, Mike. You having a sale?" The fitter smiled at Pat's astonishment as he pulled the back door open.

"You know all those things Harry keeps asking my boys to bring down?" Pat nodded.

"Well, I brought as many as I could." The Irishman bore the look of a young boy let loose in a toy store as his eyes roamed over the piled slings and other assorted equipment.

"You don't happen to have an A.G.27 block in this pirate's chest?"

"Sorry Pat, they're on back order. Should be in by the end of the week. do you need one."

"The bush in the anchor is about to fuck up. Tom reckons we should change it. We got one that Rooster fucked a few months back, but the bush and pin are a different size."

"Ok. I'll have a look at it before I go. You won't be using it today anyway. I'm going to service the tractors and the truck." This was the best news Pat could have received. Now perhaps Mark Thompson would fuck off and leave them to get on with it.

Now in a better mood, Pat answered, smiling for the first time since leaving the caravan site.

"OK, I'll get Rooster and the Wing-nut to put this stuff in the back of the truck." At that, he walked over to the open gate, placed two fingers in his mouth, and produced a piercing whistle that should have been audible in Dublin. A figure appeared from behind the mobile store. It was easily recognised as Wing-nut. Pat then reached up with both hands and pulled at both earlobes. The distinctive shape formed by his out-stretched elbows was the sign for Wing-nut. Then he put his right hand down near his crotch and vigorously pumped his hand up and down as if masturbating. Which in turn was the universal signal for Rooster? The signals were finished off with a pat on the head indicating that both of them should come to him. Satisfied that the message had been received and understood Pat returned to the rear of Mike's Morris van.

Pat's piercing whistle had attracted Mark Thompson's attention. Since changing his clothes, his time had been spent huddled over the heater vents in the Landrover cab. Both Wellington boots had been placed so that the weak flow of tepid air was directed into the long legs. Even with the engine running at high idle the heater just didn't seem to get warm. It was supposed to have been fixed at the vehicles last service and would have been had Thompson not chewed out the beleaguered mechanic. Unfortunately, he had attacked the helpless fitter before he had started on the battered Landrover. Guaranteeing that heater wouldn't be fixed until the following summer. After that, he wouldn't be able to switch off the heat at all.

A look in the rearview mirror revealed Mike O'mahony's abused van parked across the road on the grass verge. Thompson's temper flared. Here was the man responsible for the inadequate heater in the Landrover. In his tiny demented mind, Mike O'mahony suddenly became the cause of all his troubles, it was his fault, that the men hadn't been on site at eight sharp. It was his fault the Landrover had bogged down, causing him to fall flat on his face in the water filled rut, and it was his fault he was now sitting shivering over a fucking useless heater.

Throwing the door wide Mark Thompson stormed out of the cab, forgetting that he had no shoes on. The shock of the frosty grass on his bare feet further fuelled his contempt. Someone was going to pay for his discomfort, and pay heavily.

Mike spotted the angry engineer leaning back into the vehicle. A pair of black leather shoes were dropped at his feet, still laced. It was obvious that the idiot wasn't going to put them on properly. He was heading over towards them banging his feet down hard in an endeavour to get them into the tight footwear. The attempt wasn't that successful, all he really achieved was two badly skinned and painful heels. Further compounded by the fact both offending items were on the wrong feet.

"What the fuck are you doing over here? I want that first lift started." Thompson roared at Pat as he rounded the rear of Mike's van.

"Winch's fucked, Mr Thompson. Sir." Answered Pat reverting to his rural method of address.

"What do you mean the winch is fucked?"

"Ya see the thing that goes from the gearbox to the winch. It's busted. Which means the winch won't go." Pat stood looking Mark Thompson in the eye. The Irishman's face wore the same patient expression he habitually used when explaining difficult concepts to his five-year-old son. Inside he was itching to plant his fist right on the end of the arrogant man's nose.

Somewhat bemused by the lack of communication Thompson replied,

"Ok if it's broken when is it going to be fixed?"

"Well, now that depends." Pat paused looking thoughtfully towards the head fitter who had decided that for the moment it would be prudent to be rummaging through the contents of the van as if waiting for Mike O'mahony to answer. When after an extended pause the foreman failed to continue, Mark Thompson snapped,

"Well are you going to tell me today or do I have to drag it out of you?"

"Well, there's no need to be like that sir. All you need to do is ask and I'll tell you." Pat continued showing a little displeasure at being shouted at.

"Well?"

"Well what sir?" Pat answered. Again, reverting to the patient look.

"When is the thing going to be fixed?"

"What thing Sir?" Mark Thompson scowled; he was fast losing whatever patience he had so far shown. Throwing both hands up in the air in a gesture of disbelief he spat the words out one at a time.

"The fucking thing that goes from the gearbox to the winch."

"Oh. You mean the PTO shaft. Why didn't you say that in the first place? I don't have all day to stand around here talking to folk that don't know what they're talking about. Now sir, why don't you go and sit in the Landrover and get warm. You know you'll catch the death of cold walking about with no socks on. Mr O'mahony and myself will call you when the thing is fixed." Pat turned back towards Mike O'mahony, effectively dismissing the now incredulous Mark Thompson.

It was obvious that Pat wasn't going to give him the satisfaction of dressing him down in front of the Chief Mechanic. Thompson knew from bitter experience not to mess with the short balding man. His friendship with Mike Simpson gave him the edge. Well, it had in the past.

Now Mark Thompson wasn't so sure, for some time he had been associating with Nena Blenkinsopp who just happened to be the sister of the managing director. The rapidly ageing spinster had taken a shine to him at one of the director's meetings he had attended only a few months ago. Nena was employed as her brother's secretary, and fortunately for him, she had her brothers ear.

A devious and extremely ambitious man frustrated by his own failure to gain promotion, Mark had begun to manipulate Nena. She would carry stories back to her brother, and more importantly after a few pink gins would rattle on about the ins and outs of what was going on in the office. In fact, that was the very reason he had chosen to come down and push this gang on.

The board of directors in their wisdom had asked Mike Simpson why he had kept one squad working and laid off the other three. They had no concept of how weather conditions affected the different gangs. didn't they have pumps to pump the water out of the foundations? The men had wet weather gear so why weren't they working.

Thompson had seen an opportunity if he could push the only gang left working the job would finish ahead of schedule. Allowing Nena to pester her brother about promoting him over Mike Simpson. Then they would know how a company like this should be run.

Mike O'mahony had stayed buried in the back of the van while Pat was noising up the idiot engineer. It had taken him all his time not to burst out laughing at Pat's innocent rendition of a thick Irishman. Now as the bemused and infuriated Mark Thompson retreated to his Landrover, the image of his white heels clumping across the damp tarmac burned its self indelibly into his memory.

"Pat your one sassy son of a bitch. You know the bastard will be after you now."

"Ach. I was on his list anyway. He'll just put me at the top of it till someone else comes along and noises him up. The bastard hasn't got a memory big enough to hold the names of all the people that have pissed him off."

"I don't know. There's a rumour he's been shagging the MD's sister. Maybe you should watch your P's and q's." Pat grinned,

"You know to be sure, I never did learn to spell." Mike O'mahony smiled, retrieving a small box from the half-buried bottom shelf on the right-hand side of the van.

"This should be the one Pat. Give it to Harry and I'll make a start on the Truck. Can you get one of the men to give me a hand?"

At that Wing-nut and a not very happy Rooster arrived, just as the Engineers Landrover gunned away, almost clipping the rear of the truck.

"Thank fuck for that. I hope the bastard stays away." Commented Pat watching the vehicle disappear around a corner several hundred yards down the road.

"Right, you two. Put the gear Mikes brought in the back of the truck. Wing-nut, you give him a hand to service it. Rooster, once you're finished, rummage around and find some firewood, I want frost fires set next to both winches."

"How can this lazy bastard not do it?" Howled Rooster pointing indignantly at Wing-nut. Pat took a step toward the red-haired beanpole from Liverpool. His face set in a determined glare. Reluctantly Rooster turned and held his arms out ready for Mike O'mahony to load them with slings.

Pat took the small cardboard box and headed back towards the main winch. Harold and Di shouldn't be long changing the coupling. Mile O'mahony's insistence on servicing all the plant today had indeed been fortunate. The boys could relax a bit and get some much-needed tidying up done.

Chapter 14. Respite.

Pat dropped the splicer-coupling off with Harold and Di then headed towards the two riggers. Tom and Matt had rebuilt the damaged block. Other than the mounting ring being bent at ninety degrees, the block was in perfect shape. Distorted in this way, it would be impossible to get the big shackle pin through the opening in the twisted ring. Tom was reluctant to try and straighten the mangled metal. As it was, there were signs of stress on the stretched side of the loop. Any attempt to hammer it straight would likely cause the cast steel ring to fracture and fail.

The grey metal block had been manufactured in two halves. Bolted together around a six-inch diameter pulley. Each of the two sides had had a one-inch diameter phosphor bronze bush machined out to hold the stubby shaft that formed the axle for the pulley-wheel. Other than the brass bush in the centre wheel and a grease nipple recessed into the outside of each half there were no other serviceable parts in the block. The Bushes and casings were in excellent shape. Which made it even more annoying that it was unusable.

Pat clumped along the walking board doing his best to remove the last of the mud still clinging doggedly to his wellies. As he approached, Matt was finishing the bolting up of the busted pulley, while Tom had returned to searching through the piles of old ropes and slings stored inside the mobile store.

"Never Mind Tom. Mike O'mahony's going to have a look at the other one before he leaves. He has them on back order so we should get some new ones at the end of next week." Tom grunted as he jumped down to join Pat.

"Not going to do much good if that fucker fails." Said Tom frowning.

"Not going to happen Matt. Mike's going to service the plant. We won't be doing any lifting today." The big Irishman pulled a silver pocket watch from deep down in his moleskin trouser pocket.

"What about Thompson?" Tom asked hopefully.

"don't know, the bastard got a bit pissed off and drove off in a tizzy, with a bit of luck he won't be back today. Right, that's ten past ten. I think its teatime. Matt give the boys a shout."

Normally the boys would stop for ten minutes at nine-thirty, but finding Mark Thompson sitting waiting denied them their customary break. Now that he had driven off into the wilderness, hopefully never to be seen again the men could have their tea. Another sharp whistle and a lassoing motion above his head from Pat indicated to all and sundry to stop what they were doing and start for the field gate.

Mike O'mahony had the truck running, warming the big motor prior to draining oil from the sump. Wing-nut had placed a square five-gallon drum on its side under the engine. A big round hole had been cut into one side of the can, modifying it to suit the new purpose. Such cans allowed the waste oil to be collected for burning in frost fires or the large salamander heaters used to provide some heat in the cold workshop during the winter. Company policy, which was usually decided by the accountants, maintained that men worked better in the cold. Mollycoddling them in warm workshops made the men lazy and reduced their throughput. If the men wanted to get warm they should work harder.

Mike spotted the crew making their way toward the gate. He would shut down the big engine and leave it to drain while the men had their tea. On a nice clear morning like this with the sun just beginning to make its self-felt, it would be pleasant to sit and have a crack with the gang. Nodding to Wing-nut and drawing his flattened hand across his throat indicated that the lad should kill the idling engine. Like the men, Mike liked relative quiet when they sat down to eat. After four hours hard driving in the Morris van, the chief engineer welcomed the chance for a break.

It took him thirty seconds to remove the drain plug from the warm sump. A stream of hot dirty black oil gushed from the plughole on the bottom of the metal sump-pan, collecting in the modified metal can below. A quick inspection showed the magnetic plug to be relatively free of metal fillings. Harold regularly changed the engine oil and filter element, unlike most of the company trucks, unless there was a problem this one never built up many fillings. Good oil prevented ware on the important parts of the engine.

The truck rocked on its heavy-duty leaf springs as one after another the men clambered up the foot-holds cut into the dropped tailgate. Mike retreated from under the truck, wiping the warm black oil from his hands with a dirty rag. Placing the drain-plug on top of the big metal bumper the chief mechanic made his way to the Morris and retrieved his bag. Returning to join the rest of the men in the back of the lorry.

Rooster appeared at the back of the truck ready to pull himself up. Pat, sitting at the back, stuck out his foot barring the outcast from joining the rest of the crew.

"You can sit in the cab. And don't touch anything." Roosters retort was instantaneous.

"What you blaming me for? I'm not the fucking idiot that got his hand caught in the gearbox." Pat glared down at the wiry Scouser

"One more word out of you and I'll be looking for a new climber. Understand" Pat's voice bore a threat that even Rooster knew not to argue with.

"Now fuck off and sit in the cab. One fart and you're fired." At that Pat throw Roosters canvas bag down to him and turned back to Mike. Seething, Rooster turned away. As far as he was concerned this day couldn't end quickly enough.

Mike looked at Pat inquiringly.

"That stupid fucker stuck his foot down in front of the gear stick, Harry missed a change and the bitch jammed herself in third gear again. When Davie was trying to free the selector, Rooster hit the starter switch. Davies' hand got stuck between the two lay-shafts. We had to take him to hospital. That's why we were late on site this morning."

"Is he ok?" Mike had developed a worried look.

"The sister told me she didn't think there were any bones broken, but his hand is pretty bruised. Might be a few weeks before its healed properly." Mike silently heaved a sigh of relief. Accidents were common in most of the gangs, but unusual in this one. He also realised that there was more to the story than the brief few sentences that Pat had given him.

Mike relaxed; Pat would fill him in on the details later. There was an unspoken rule that work was never discussed at teatime. This brief ten-minute break gave the men a chance to relate to things other than work. The two topics of conversation this morning were, Davies accident and how long it would be before the Welshman would return to work. This was quickly dealt with then they moved onto Harold's news.

"You got a name picked Harry?" Di asked. Harold nodded; Di had been the first to congratulate him earlier. All the men knew that Di and his wife Helen loved children. On the sites, the couple were the normal repository for lost children. Helen's caravan was always the first place to look when a child went missing.

Helen had lived all her life in the little Welsh village of Bethesda. Eventually taking a job as a primary school teacher in the local school. Even as a teenager it was obvious that the shapely young woman had problems. An abnormal growth in her uterus had meant a hysterectomy, forever denying her the ability to have children of her own. Being of practical Welsh stock, the plucky young girl had decreed that if she couldn't have children of her own she would dedicate her life to helping other peoples. First by becoming a teacher then later after she had married Di a foster parent for extremely troubled children. Now she had two young orphaned girls. Both had been severely abused by close family members. Leaving them with deep psychological problems.

The nine-year-old twins had become a problem for the local authorities in East Anglia. Several sites back. A chance meeting with a local social worker had allowed Helen and Di to foster the twins. Within weeks of joining the Welsh couple, there had been a significant improvement in the girl's behaviour. So much so that even allowing for the transient nature of their lifestyle it was deemed important that the children stay with Helen and Di. The local authorities had dumped the girls on them, hoping that when they moved on the hassle associated with the troublesome children went with them. Now apart from informing the authorities in East Anglia each time they moved, there was little contact between the couple and the social services.

Di had been brought up in the mining village of Abervan. following his five brothers into the mines. Several years later the terrible conditions underground had brought on chronic bronchitis, laying him off permanently. The doctors had advised him to move away from the valleys and find a better climate to recuperate. So, when he was well enough his mother packed him off to live with an aunt in Bethesda in North Wales.

It wasn't long before the clean fresh air of North Wales had a healing effect on the young Di Jones. Although his aunt suspected that the young schoolteacher he was courting had much to do with his recovery.

Time passed, and the couple were married, unfortunately, Di was unable to find much work in the local area. A chance meeting brought Di and Pat together in the small village post office. As usual, the postmistress, an ageing old crone who insisted on sharing every morsel of gossip with each customer would treat each as if they were the only one in the shop, stretching the time spent in the queue from a few minutes to around half an hour.

Di had been posting some letters for Helen, while Pat had been trying to post the weekly time-sheets. Spotting the big stranger in the queue, the old woman had assumed he was from across the border. Fiercely patriotic and having a burning hatred of all Englishmen. The old crone had seen to it that the two women in front of Pat got an extra helping of scandal. Of course, delivered in rapid Welsh denying Pat any hope of understanding their conversations. Even Di who had been brought up in the very heart of Wales was having some difficulty in keeping up with the rapid-fire conversation between the old woman and her customers. Unlike their woman folk, most Welshmen are social beings and Di was no exception. It wasn't long before the two men had struck up a conversation. Neither man brave enough to try testing the patience of the village matriarch.

One thing led to another and Di ended up working on the erection gang. Even though his weak chest stopped him working at height, Pat quickly found that he and Davie Jones worked well together. Serving his time as general dogs-body, when the junior winch-man left the gang he was the natural choice to assist his good-natured countryman.

Both he and Helen had quickly become accustomed to the roving lifestyle that came with his job. Now that it was almost certain that the twins would be allowed to stay with them, both were content. Hardly ever mourning the fact that they could never have any children of their own.

"Going to call him Daniel, if it's a boy and Danielle if it's a girl," Harold replied.

"You're lucky, it took that bugger of mine three weeks after Lisa was born before she settled on a name. Even at the registry office the bloke behind the counter nearly chucked us out." Said Matt, causing a ripple of laughter around the men.

"So, when is she due?" asked Matt.

"Well, the doc told her she's about four months, so that would make it around." Harold paused mental arithmetic had never been his best subject.

"February or March." The young Cornish-man chipped in. Everyone in the gang knew he was shit hot with numbers. Changing the subject Harold started on a new track,

"What about you Gerry. You got a hot little Cornish lass tucked away someplace?" The young man blushed. When it came to girls, he was a complete disaster. His tongue tied in knots, his palms became sweaty and his heart raced. The years of constant slagging about his odd looks had driven his self-esteem down deeper than any mine that the two Welshmen had ever dug coal in. There was only one woman who had ever treated him with respect. Elsie his stepmother, whom he seldom talked about. Gerry had learned early never to say anything in front of Rooster. The Liverpudlian's, razor sharp and insistent mocking could become almost unbearable. Unlike the other men who would normally explode, Gerry would just shut up and tried to let it wash over his back.

"What's that fucker Thompson up to Mike?" Pat asked saving Gerry from answering.

"Don't know. There's a rumour going around that he's been seen with Nena Blenkinsopp, you know the managing director's sister. Scuttlebutt has it that he's leading her right up the garden path." Pat grunted and answered, stuffing a huge empire biscuit into his mouth.

"It's the only way that fucker will get a promotion. The bitch must be nearsighted, going by the size of his shrivelled little dick this morning she can't be very fussy. You should have seen him, Mike. Stripped down, bollock naked, trying to dry himself off with a hand towel. It the coppers had come along he would have been arrested." The men laughed, the idea of Mark Thompson being carted off in handcuffs, ballock naked appealed to them all.

Chapter 15. The Return.

Pat cocked his head, listening to the sound of an approaching vehicle. It had the familiar Landrover sound.

"Speak of the devil." Said, Pat, as the D6 Landrover pulled around them, stopping on the other side of the field gate. Barely seconds elapsed before the driver's door violently swung open. Mark Thompson boldly jumped out, sporting a brand-new pair of black Wellington's. He still wore the black suit that he had changed into after his earlier dunking. It was obvious that the angry and bemused man that had left so hurriedly half an hour ago had gone. Now he had a bone in his teeth. Walking briskly to the back of the truck he stood, hands on his hips and barked.

"I have just been talking to the managing director of this cowboy outfit. He's given me full authority to get this pylon erected as I see fit. Anyone failing to comply with my orders is to be sacked on the spot. Is that clear?"

Pat glared back at him, not quite sure how he should reply. It was Mike O'mahony that answered,

"Well, you better just run back and complain to him. I'm down here to service all the plant on this site and that will take me all day. And by the way. Be sure to mention my name. Michael O'mahony. do you want me to spell it out for you?" There was no mistaking the iron in the chief mechanics voice. He meant what he said.

"I'm in charge of safety on these sites, and until I'm satisfied, nothing moves. Now get back into your Landrover and get the fuck out of here."

Mark Thompson's face turned red with rage,

"I, I've never been spoken to in this manner by a grease monkey and I'm not about to start now. You're fired." Mike stared him in the face, emptying the dregs of his tea out with a quick flick of the wrist, narrowly missing the irate civil engineer. Slowly and very deliberately Mike put his cup back on top of his vacuum flask and replaced it in his knapsack. Turning, he dismounted the truck and turned to face his advisory.

Mark Thompson was a full head taller than the chief mechanic, and perhaps five stone heavier. The smaller man glared up, his voice almost a growl,

"Let's get some things straight.

Number one.

I am your superior. Not the MD, his responsibilities lay in dealing with the board and the financial responsibilities of the company. He never gets himself involved in the day-to-day workings at site level.

Second.

You are only a junior civil engineer, employed by the company. Your job is to see that the Pylon gets put together as it is in the plans. You have nothing to do with the erection. You don't have the responsibility or knowledge to run a piss up in a brewery let alone organise a gang of skilled men. That's Pat's job and he is very good at It." Each point was accentuated by Mikes right-hand index finger prodding the larger man's sternum. Pushing him back a step each time.

It was obvious which way the David and Goliath confrontation was going. Each point drove the livid engineer back toward the open Landrover door. Thompson was like most bullies, a coward at heart. Had he had an audience of his peers then the battle might have been different. Here the whole gang was watching, even Rooster who had jumped out of the cab when the Landrover pulled up.

Mike continued to berate the angry and by now quite worried man. The chief mechanic's knowledge of the workings and responsibilities of the different grades of employees was beginning to sink in. By the time he decided to jump back into the Landrover and raced off in the direction the jeep was facing. Mike had almost brought his self-esteem down to his knees. Leaving the smaller man standing confidently with his hand on hips as the vehicle disappeared along the road.

The confident expression changed to a scowl. There was no telling what mischief the arrogant fool had caused. If he had been talking to the MD god knows what foolish notions had been placed in the vacuum between his ears. At board level, most of the members were wealthy men, long separated from the reality and day-to-day working of a corporation this size. Even worse their attitudes and working experiences had been formed under a King long since dead. Some of them would even be old enough to remember the reign of Queen Victoria.

Mark Thompson's Oxford background and arrogant attitude would fit right in with most of the out of date thinking, rife at that level of corporate responsibility. This couldn't be allowed to go any further. Much as he wished to spend the rest of the day on site. His better judgement forced him to change his mind. Turning back to Pat and the men who had joined him on the road, he spat aggressively at the ground and addressed the ganger.

"I think I better get hold of Mike Simpson, there's no telling what damage that bastard has done. Where's the nearest phone, Pat?"

"It's at a crossroad two miles down this road." Pat pointed back along the road in the direction Mark Thompson had come.

"Right, can you get Harry to finish the truck and do the services on the two Counties. I'll be back as soon as I can. However, there's no telling where he is. If the bastard comes back, I'll be at the phone. Stall him." Mike turned and headed for the Morris van wearing his most grim expression.

The men turned back to Pat. Waiting for confirmation from their own boss.

"You heard him, let's get back to work. Harry, you finished with that prop-shaft yet?"

Harold shook his head, replying,

"No, not yet, we're having trouble getting the bent spanner off the yoke."

"Right, leave that to Rooster. If anyone can fuck it up it's him." Snarled Pat looking directly at Rooster.

"Fuck you, get Peter perfect here to fix it." Snapped Rooster, thumbing defiantly in Harold's direction.

"Listen, you scouse git. That's you're fucking spanner wrapped around that shaft. You get the fucking thing off. Without fucking it up. do you understand?" Roosters eardrums were in danger of collapsing, Pat had leaned over close to Roosters face, bellowing his request.

"No need to shout. I'm not deaf" Replied Rooster in an indignant manner, just defiant enough to register his disgust at being given this task. While not incurring further wrath from the gang boss.

"Right lads get the rest of this stuff stowed in the back of the truck. No need to drag it across the field." Instructed Pat kicking the pile of equipment that had been unloaded onto the grass verge behind the Morris van.

Harold picked up the filter boxes that Mike had left sitting on top of a five-gallon drum of Shell oil.

"Gerry will you bring the can of oil over and get the filler jug from the County." Wing-nut nodded and carried the heavy can over to the front of the truck. Then trudged across the field towards the big winch engine along with the rest of the squad.

Over the next half hour, the men settled down to their assigned tasks. Even Rooster succeeded in removing the twisted spanner from the prop shaft, and for once without doing any further damage. Harry and Wing-nut finished servicing the four tonner, and started across the field towards the main winch. Di Jones had spent his time greasing both sets of winch gear and the steering on the truck. Tom and Matt had settled down to rigging the first of the six arms that would be winched up into position the next day, weather permitting. While Pat stood over the reluctant Rooster.

None of them noticed the D6 Landrover pulling up at the gate. This time the vehicle had come quietly back down the road, pulling in front of the four-toner where the hedge was high enough to hide the grey hard top. Nor did the occupant rush to get out of the jeep.

It had been a move carefully calculated to lull the crew into a false sense of security. By the time Mark Thompson was noticed he would be on top of them. Moreover, this time, there wouldn't be any meddling grease monkey to get in his way.

In his earlier phone call to Nena, he hadn't actually talked to the MD After explaining his situation, The woman had instantly taken her lover's side. Noting down the phone number of the call-box, she told him to sit tight and wait. Indicating that she would call him back in a few minutes.

Nigel Blenkinsopp had been in a meeting with two of the company directors. He was in the middle of a power struggle, that would ultimately decide whether he remained on as MD or was replaced by a younger man, almost half his age. The fight had been bitter, Nigel was fighting for his life, and things were not looking good.

Nena had knocked and entered quietly, making her way around behind his desk before bending to whisper quietly in his ear. For a moment he listened intently. Not wishing to show anger either towards his sister or in front of the two directors, Nigel fought to maintain a detached and formal attitude. Nodding appropriately, as he would have Nena brought any important message before him.

However, he was in fact seething. He hated the arrogant fool his sister had been courting for the last few months. The man was a bore. Having to put on a polite face in his company was a strain that was fast becoming unbearable. Here was a chance to rid himself of the fool. He had no doubt that given an inch the ambitious idiot would over-state his authority. If he called this one properly, a report would find its way to his desk around the end of the following week. With luck, it would state that the overconfident moron had been sacked. Even better, in Nena's eyes, it wouldn't be him at fault.

Nena stood up waiting patiently for her brother's instructions. Nigel fained a thoughtful look as if contemplating a major problem. Then turning back to his two visitors simply answered,

"Tell him to exercise his authority with appropriate force." Then he dismissed Nena, quickly falling back into the conversation with his two colleagues.

By the time the simple sentence had been enhanced and massaged to suit her needs, Nena Blenkinsopp had literally given her lover the keys to the company. Inflating his already oversized opinion of his responsibilities within the organisation.

By the time he had returned to the erection site, first detouring to purchase a new pair of Wellington's. The indignities suffered earlier had been replaced by an iron-clad idea that he was invincible. He would show that ignorant mick and the incompetent mechanic. Before the day was out he would have both their hides.

Nena's rendition of her brother's instructions had been weighted heavily towards promotion if this operation could be brought in ahead of schedule. After all, it would be a feather in his cap when dealing with the board.

On the way back to the site Mark Thompson had run several possible scenarios through his mind, all of them involved him being appointed to the board of directors. As far as he was concerned there could only be one outcome. Even the old and useless head mechanic would finally have to bow before him. At that thought, his pleasure turned to gloating. Now finally he would be able to achieve some measure of revenge for the indignities the balding little fool had heaped on him over the past few years.

"Yes, he would have his revenge." The thought pleased him immensely.

Nothing in his being had prepared him for Mike O'mahony's retort. The third generation Irishman had simply hammered him down. Bowling him over with fact after fact concerning company structure and management procedures. Oh! He had been prepared for a fight, but not this. The chief fitter hadn't even raised his voice, but his points had been delivered with astounding accuracy. Each one hammered home with sheer logic. The same procedural logic he himself used when bullying junior members of the civil engineering staff. However, Mike had delivered it without the sneering arrogance he himself would use. There was no evidence of ego in Mike O'mahony's delivery. Only cold clear logic.

Once again he had retreated from the site, this time seething from his own failure to conquer Mike O'mahony. Bewilderment turned to loathing. Twisting his already battered thought processes into an even more deranged and unstable state. Now he was trapped. On one side he would lose face with Nena and her brother, forever barring him from any chance of promotion to the board. On the other side, Mike O'mahony had defaced his authority in front of the squad. That would be his final mistake.

Thompson hadn't gone far, there was a small wood about half a mile from the field gate. Pulling the Landrover into a small passing place that sheltered below the overhanging trees. Autumn had come slowly this year; The mild wet weather had delayed the annual colour change. Where there would normally be rich browns and gold's, there was still a fair spattering of yellow-green leaves. However, even they would begin to fall when the first high winds shook the branches clean ready for winter.

A dirt track disappeared into the trees. Logic told him that it would lead into a field where he would be able to observe the erection site. Gathering up his binoculars, he jumped out of the jeep, climbed over the rickety gate, and followed the unused track through the wood.

The trees sat on top of a gentle rise with the road running down one side and a field on the other. The track showed little sign of being used. The long grass grew down the centre and along both sides, leaving only the barest rut where a tractors wheels had compacted the dirt track, denying the grass a chance to grow. The grass was still soaking wet, splashing up from his wellies, soaking his dark suit trousers. However, unlike his earlier dunking this time, only his determined resolve to obtain revenge at all cost prevailed.

The track twisted and turned around mature oaks, intermingled with ash, beech, and elm, some of who may have stood there for centuries. After about a hundred yards, a second gate bounded on either side by thick unkempt hedges led out into a meadow that rolled gently down towards the barley field where the unfinished pylon stood.

In his own mind, Thompson was now the great white hunter, setting up his unsuspecting prey for the kill.

Cautiously, holding himself to the hedge at the left-hand side of the gate, the binoculars were brought to bear. First the gate, where Mike O'mahony's Morris van should have been parked. It wasn't there, a quick scan back along the road towards the phone box, showed the little brown van racing along the lanes well over a mile away. The fitter must be worried.

A sneer formed at the thought. It would take time for him to track down Mike Simpson. Who would then have to get to Nigel Blenkinsop? Nena was an excellent personal secretary. It would be a long time before Mike Simpson would be talking to the MD. Now that his plans were finally coming together, even the regional manager wouldn't dare confront him.

The men had dispersed, the ignorant Jock and the deformed Cornishman were working around the truck, probably finishing off the incompetent fitter's job. He reserved a particularly evil grin for Pat and Rooster, who had made their way across the field and seemed to be working on some kind of shaft. Pats build and Roosters flaming red hair easily allowing him to distinguish the two. The two riggers had preceded to one of the arms and were busily rigging it for a lift.

"Good." he thought. That fitted in well with his hastily formed plans. If everything was ready, there could be no excuses for not getting on with the lift. Now if he could time it right before that Jock bastard disabled anymore plant things would fall into place.

Chapter 16. No Escape.

"Now if you worked like that all the time, I wouldn't have to shout at you so much," Pat told Rooster in an almost mild manner. The young man could make a good job of things especially when he was aloft. It was as if there was a loose wire flapping about in his brain. depending on which way the wind blew the wire would earth out, instantly turning a fairly decent individual into a raving dangerous lunatic.

Like most men who liked to get things done Pat found it difficult to stand back and watch a less competent man struggle with a difficult task. Today was no exception. Rooster had all the grace of a flying slug of sea-gull shit. Twice the long metal pinch bar, he was using to pry the twisted spike free, slipped, almost landing the lad flat on his face. Pat didn't know whether to laugh at the comic antics or roar in anger at the frustration caused by the lad's ineptness with that particular tool. Like most people who are naturally right handed, Pat found watching left-handers like Rooster extremely difficult. Further adding to the frustration, he was feeling.

This morning, after all, that had happened Pat forced himself into being patient and showing Harold how it should be done. If his friend was finally going to take up the reigns and run his own squad, then Pat should set a good example. The big man felt responsible for the events that led directly to Davies accident. There was no way around it the accident had been caused by his determination to punish Rooster for his bad temper and disgusting habits. The boy didn't know any better. However, Pat did.

Harold and Wing-nut had joined Pat and Rooster, just as the last bit of the offending spanner had been prised free. The Spicer coupling had still to be removed and replaced now that the bent spanner wasn't hindering the extraction. The tools that were required were a vice, two suitable sockets, and a pair of circlip pliers. Most of which Harold had brought over with him.

Because most repairs had to be done on site, both county tractors had vices mounted on solid bits of their frames. Even the four-tonner had one hidden under the bench seats which lined both sides of the truck bed. The four men had gathered around the vice mounted on the large ballast weight at the front of the main winch engine. Because of the heavy construction of the shaft, it took Pat and Rooster to support the free end while with Wing-nut's help Harold pressed out the first two of the four bearing caps.

Then they had to press the new coupling into the yoke of the short drive end. Once that had been done the process was repeated, adding the now half assembled drive end to the main shaft. Again, it took two of them to support the heavy shaft while Harold and Wing-nut carefully pressed the bearing caps into place. With the assistance of the other men, the whole operation took less than twenty minutes.

"I trust that now that shaft has been fixed you are ready to make the first lift." Pat whipped around to find Mark Thompson, standing behind them. On his face a particularly self-satisfied smirk that instantly told the big Irishman that this time there was no escaping. Had Mike still been there it would have been impossible for the engineer to counter his orders. Now using the very same logic that Mike had so efficiently chased this same arrogant bastard from the site. Pat and the men would have to accede to his commands, now that he was indeed the senior man on site.

"Well sir we could do that, but Mr O'mahony has instructed that we service the two winches today." Mark Thompson looked down at the mud caked around his new wellies, a self-satisfied smirk on his face.

"And where is he now?"

"Gone to the phone. Sir." Answered Pat maintaining the cap-in-hand rural attitude that experience had taught him was indeed the best way to deal with fools like this.

"Well, I can assure you he won't be back today. Now can we get this fucking shambles on the road." Pat hated to be beaten. Still, he had one last ace up his sleeve.

"Yes sir, but."

"Well spit it out, man."

"Yes, sir. We're a man down today. It wouldn't be safe to lift the gear today. No Sir, it wouldn't."

"So, who's so indispensable that the rest of you can't work without him?" His voice was loaded with contempt.

"Davie, sir. Davie Jones. He's our senior winch man, sir."

"Well, you'll just have to do it yourself. Won't you. I will direct the operation. You will operate the winch. do you understand?" Pat was trapped, he could operate the winch, like most of the ganger's he had come up through the ranks doing all the jobs on site. It was one of the reasons none of the men could fleece him when it came to excuses.

"Yes, sir I can do that. But are you sure you can direct the lift, sir?" Pat was now on very dangerous ground.

"Well if an idiot like you can do it I certainly can." There was no hiding the contempt in the engineer's tone.

"Yes, sir. If you say so, sir." Pat turned away fuming, determined not to show the fool how he felt. Now they were in it, right up to their proverbial necks.

"Harry, how long should it take to put this shaft back in?" Pat asked. Trying to deflect the conversation.

"You've got ten minutes, after that if this winch isn't hooked up and lifting that arm you're all sacked." Mark Thompson's tone had the words, "I dare you." Woven through.

"Yes, Sir. We can do dat. Can't we Harry?" Harold nodded. The look in Pat's eye told him to play along. With luck, Mike O'mahony would be back shortly. Pat had to find a way to slow things down, without being obvious,

"Harry, you go and get your gear set out for going up-top. Rooster you and Gerry put the shaft back in. Mr Thompson here will show you how to do it." I'll go and get the rest of the men ready. In one deft move, Pat had put the civil engineer in charge of the repair. Effectively anchoring him to the area around the main winch. He was counting on Rooster holding up the proceedings for some time, giving Mike O'mahony time to get back. He felt sorry for Gerry who would undoubtedly bear some of the madman's wrath. However, the stoic Cornish-man was more than a match for Thompson's bullying tactics. The lad was just where he could do the most good. Every word coming from the dangerous fool's lips would be engraved indelibly in Gerry's memory. The thought brought a faint smile to Pats face as he and Harold walked away along the boards towards Di and the two riggers.

Had everything been in order Pat had no doubt they would have lifted at least two of the arms on this side of the pylon. Probably all three. The delay caused by Davies accident and the loss of an experienced man. Had certainly put his initial goals in jeopardy. Mike O'mahony's arrival and the knowledge that the regional manager wasn't expecting them to do any lifting for at least a few days had changed his perspective on the planned tasks. Between Harold and Mike, the plant would have been in tip-top condition by the end of the day. Now that much-needed maintenance was not going to happen.

Pat called Tom, Matt, and Di Jones over to the mobile store and informed them of the change of plans. Tom was not happy,

"Pat that block on the anchor should be changed before we try and lift the first arm. You know the score as well as I do if it locks near the top the strain on the rope might snap it. Anyway, we will need to run up the ropes before starting the lift." Pat knew that Tom was right. If the block froze, which was the most likely type of failure, they could end up with an arm hanging out in mid-air. Today that wouldn't be much of a problem, but if a wind got up it would start swinging. There was no telling what might happen if the ropes failed. The heavy arm could fall to the ground damaging the other two. Or worse.

Tom changed tack,

"Who's going to work the control winch?"

"I am," Pat responded.

"Thank fuck for that. For a minute I thought that tosser was going to try it himself." Tom looked relieved. All the men knew and trusted each other's skills. Having a stranger in one of the more skilled jobs, tended to make them nervous.

"The bastards certainly arrogant enough to think he could do it himself." Interceded Matt.

"No, he's going to do my job." Answered Pat.

"Jesus, Pat, he hasn't got a clue." Snapped Di Jones. during a lift, both Davie and himself depended on Pats hand signals to get the lift into position. Then Harold and rooster climbed up and landed the arm. After years of working together, the two men had almost become an extension of Pat himself. Now suddenly the most important corner of the triangle was going to be replaced by a man with little knowledge and none of the skills required for the job.

"I don't like it either. So today we play it by the numbers. Let's not have any more accidents. OK. Leave the bastard to me. By the sound of it Roosters giving him a piece of his mind. Maybe he'll get pissed off again and fuck off." All of them knew the last statement was a forlorn hope.

Over at the big County, the air was getting blue. Rooster had just succeeded in jamming the shaft in the control rods that passed under the console and down to the brake control housing just above the main transfer gearbox. Wing-nut had been guiding the shaft down into the cavity when Rooster who was holding the top end of the PTO shaft caught his finger between the spicer coupling and the yoke. There was barely enough pressure to cause a black nail, but Rooster howled in agony, dropping the shaft. Wing-nut had barely managed to stop the rouge assembly from falling onto Mark Thompson's feet.

There was little room on the small platform for two people to manoeuvre the heavy shaft into the casing. Mark Thompson's twenty-five stone bulk left no room on the platform. At six foot four, the big man didn't really look fat. His height and weight coupled with the extremely unpleasant attitude that accompanied them had always given him the edge in face-to-face confrontations.

"Pick up that shaft you fucking idiot," Thompson growled at Rooster.

"Fuck you." Shouted Rooster, nursing the injured digit.

"Get out of my way." Ordered Thompson, pulling Rooster towards the metal ladder leading up to the platform. Nearly sending the lighter man flying.

"Who the fuck do you think you are?" Howled Rooster indignantly. Catching the handles on either side of the ladder. A move that prevented him from falling off the big machine.

Mark Thompson turned back on Rooster, snarling at the angry climber.

"Get out of my way you fucking moron. Or you're sacked." Rooster made to snap a sarcastic reply but choked it as Mark Thompson's outstretched right index finger stopped just under the point of his nose.

"One more word. Just one more word. do you understand?" Even Rooster knew when it was pointless to continue. The look of pure evil on the civil engineer's red face sent shivers down his spine. deciding that discretion was the better part of valour. Rooster hurriedly descended the ladder and made directly for Pat and the other men.

"That bastards crazy Pat. He nearly pushed me off the fucking platform into the mud." He bellowed indignantly, interrupting Pat.

"What did you do to deserve that I wonder." Answered Pat sarcastically.

"I jammed my finger in the coupling. Look" Rooster held up his index finger, which did indeed look as if the tip was swelling. Then just as suddenly the boy's mood changed

"Nearly dropped the heavy end on his fucking toes. ha-ha" The little snigger at the end told Pat that the injury had been part of a ploy to annoy Thompson.

"Where's Gerry?" asked Pat looking back towards the winch. Neither he nor Thompson were visible. No doubt Wing-nut would try and stretch out the time it would take to re-insert the heavy shaft.

"Giving that tosser a hand to put the shaft back on." At that Pat saw Wing-nut stand up abruptly, pushing himself away from the centre-console and the determined engineer. The lad looked skywards and blew. Edging his way to the ladder and safety.

In his anger Thompson had dragged Wing-nut out of the way, reaching down into the tangle of rods and ropes. His first attempt had failed, resulting in a long tear down the sleeve of his black suit jacket, exposing the white shirt below.

Thompson was so intent on getting the PTO shaft back into place, he hardly noticed the damage to the garment. Wing-nut had been forced to jump over the man's writhing form, making it safely to the ladder. Then a particularly violent twist sent both of the engineer's feet out over the ladder, nearly knocking Gerry to the ground. Fortunately, the lad found safety by swinging deftly onto the huge rear tractor tyre.

Even thirty yards away the assembled men could hear Thompson roar in anger as he tried in vane to re-mount the five-foot-long drive shaft. A simple job when done by two men co-coordinating with each other, it was almost impossible for one man to balance the extending shaft and manipulate the couplings at either end.

To Mark Thompson, it was at first glance a simple operation. All they had to do was slip the shaft down into the cavity. Then manhandle it into position. However, gravity had taken over pulling the slightly lighter inner portion of the shaft out. Instead of five feet of heavy metal, the extended assembly now measured over seven feet. The exposed inner section which was covered in thick sticky grease made it even more difficult to hold onto.

When the realisation that he couldn't manage this feat on his own finally penetrated. A rush of humiliation sent him into a rage. Kicking and screaming at the jammed shaft. Four feet of which still protruded from the floor of the platform. Wing-nut who had never seen a man in such a state jumped down from the huge tyre and ran towards Pat and the rest. ducking as anything movable had been thrown from the platform in whatever direction Thompson happened to be pointing. The man's anger and indignities were further boosted by the pain from his first full force kick at the shaft.

The hastily purchased Wellington boots had been destined for farm workers and unlike the heavier models used by the construction industry, didn't have steel toe-caps. Thompson's violent rage had prevented him from considering the consequences of attacking metal with the soft-toed boots. The sudden intense pain from the first kick had set him hopping around the platform in agony. Waves of anger and pain alternated between seething hatred for the inanimate tractor and indignity caused by the hurt to his anything but delicate, size twelve foot.

Chapter 17. The devil and the deep blue sea.

Pat and the rest of the men retreated behind the mobile store as the crazed civil engineer hopped around hammering at the console with a three-foot-long monkey wrench.

"What the fuck are we going to do Pat?" Asked Gerry, in an uncharacteristic outburst. It was obvious that the quiet Cornish-man was scared, Gerry had never been known to swear.

"I don't know, Gerry." Said Pat, laying a hand on the lad's shoulder. As much for his own benefit as to reassure the boy. Both men flinched as a spike impacted on the metal side of the mobile store.

"This bastard is going to kill someone." Tom volunteered to no-one in particular. Somehow voicing the opinions of the assembled crew with the exception of Rooster.

The fool had stuck his red head out far enough to see what the maniac was doing. Ducking in and out excitedly while giving a running commentary on the antics of the deranged man.

Pat was worried, basically, he had two choices. He could walk off the site taking the rest of the men with him. Few would blame them for refusing to work under such conditions. But the same people would undoubtedly blacklist them all. It could be a long time before any of them worked again. Word got around fast and he was not about to put a perfectly good gang of men onto the dole.

In some ways, the second choice was the harder of the two. Now that the civil engineer had shown his true colours, working with him around was going to affect the men. One reason the squad did so well was the unspoken trust that had developed. It was like Pats hand signals, barely visible to the untrained eye, but unmistakable in their impact.

The men jumped as a sudden loud bang sounded from the tin roof of their makeshift shelter. The sound of a metal socket rattling down the corrugated sheet made them all move hurriedly away from the store. After a few seconds, it dropped off, landing right next to Roosters left foot.

"The bastard." Shouted Rooster as he bent to pick up the round metal object. Pat stared in horror as the lanky Liverpudlian, stepped out, hurling the silver socket back towards the winch. Another of the lad's unfortunate talents was his ability to hit moving targets with a thrown object. Most days there would be several dead Rabbits in the back of the truck as a testament to the lad's prowess as a thrower.

The last thing Pat wanted was Rooster to get involved in a hurling match with the deranged man. There was another indignant howl from the direction of the winch. Had Rooster had found his mark? Two of the men hurriedly grabbed Rooster pulling him back out of harm's way. The big Irishman winched waiting for the expected retort.

A sudden and almost complete silence reigned.

"Oh fuck you've killed the bastard." Said Matt quietly, gingerly peeking around the side of the store. Not wishing to expose any part of himself to further danger.

"Where is he?" asked Matt as the others joined him on both sides of the metal store.

"Stay here. Keep that eejit quiet." Ordered Pat, as he carefully moved out from the van, expending his restricted field of view. Thompson was nowhere to be seen. Cautiously the big ganger made his way towards the winch. It was obvious that the men were struggling to keep the excited Rooster out of sight.

"Mr Thompson. Would you be alright now?" Pat called as he cautiously approached the winch.

"And why wouldn't I be?" Asked Thompson, appearing from behind the huge tractor tyre on the far side of the winch. The right arm of his suit jacket was torn from wrist to elbow, allowing the once white shirt underneath to show. It was obvious that he was limping.

"You seemed to be a little-upset sir. Would you be alright now Sir?" Thompson looked a little dazed. As he turned, Pat could see a cut high on his forehead. A bulge was beginning to form around the trickle of blood. It wasn't clear how the deranged man had acquired the cut. It was plausible that it had been from the socket launched by Rooster. However, it could just as easily been caused by the angry man bumping his forehead in his haste to refit the shaft.

"I think so," Thompson replied dreamily. Pat recognised the opportunity to rid themselves of this dangerous fool. If he could herd the engineer back over to his Landrover, with a bit of luck the dazed man would drive off into the sunset. At least over there they would be free from his angry outbursts.

"That's a nasty cut on your head, sir. I think you should go and sit in your jeep for a while. At least till you get your breath back." Pat accepted the bemused stare as acceptance of his suggestion. Calling Matt and Tom over he instructed them to help Mr Thompson back to his car. They weren't out of the woods yet.

"Harry you and Gerry get that shaft fitted. Rooster, you keep an eye out for him coming back across the field. I don't want to be caught out again. Thank fuck we were working when that bastard crept up on us." Pat looked hopefully across the field towards the road. If only Mike O'mahony would return. Then perhaps some sort of order would be maintained. Thompson was a dangerous man to have on site. In his present state, there was no telling what he might do.

The knock on the head had certainly calmed him down for the moment. Allowing Tom and Matt to lead him back to his vehicle, like a puppy on a leash. However, there was no telling how long the docile state might last. One thing was sure by the end of the day he was going to have one big lump on his forehead.

Another possibility was that the knock was serious enough to render him unconscious if left alone in the jeep. Nor would it be a good idea to let him drive. God knows what might happen if he blacked out behind the wheel. No, unless Mike O'mahony came back they would have to nurse the arrogant bastard until it was clear he was fit to drive. Reluctantly Pat set off towards the gate. He would have to risk the fool's wrath once again. This time hiding the Landrover keys.

"Would you be alright, Mr Thompson?" Asked Pat leaning in the passenger's door of the jeep. Mark Thompson seemed to have recovered some of his composure, however, he still wore a faraway expression around his eyes. Pat swiftly pulled the key from the ignition switch on the dashboard. Taking the chance when Thompson was looking out of the window for some unknown reason.

Every now and again he would place the flat of his left hand on the bulge forming on his forehead, screwing up his face in an effort to clear the grey mist that accompanied the pulsating pain in his head. The trickle of blood from the bump had congealed, leaving an orange-red stain where he had done his best to wipe it clear.

Tom and Matt left him to Pat. Neither of them felt safe around the big man. The ganger would be more than a match for him in his dazed state. Pat Tried again.

"Will you be needing anything, Mr Thompson?" This time he got a response. Suddenly any trace of bewilderment had gone. Mark Thompson glared back at him then growled.

"Enough of this. I want that lift started by the time I get over there. Now fuck off back to the rest of those morons and get that winch going."

"Yes, sir Mr Thompson, I'll do that." Pat was fuming, it seemed that the engineer was now back in control of his faculties and was still intent on forcing the lift. It would take a miracle to get rid of him now.

Pat trudged back across the field. It was obvious to the rest of the team that things hadn't gone well. That could only mean one thing. Thompson was back to normal. As he neared the main winch engine, Pat made a lassoing motion above his head, indicating that he wanted all the men to gather round.

Harold and Wing-nut dismounted the platform. The shaft had been refitted, and the covers were back in place, however, Harold wasn't happy.

"Pat it looks like that idiot bent some of the brake control rods when he was banging about in there. You know how delicate the adjustment is on them. If they're not right the brake might not hold." Pat Frowned.

"Dam! Which side?"

"The control winch." The ganger leaned back against the big tractor tyre.

"Bastard." Pat's single retort, spat out with all the force of a rifle bullet summed up the way the full squad felt. Looking from man to man Pat wrestled with his conscience. If he refused to work with the civil engineer on site then it was possible that none of these men, including himself, would be able to find work for a long, long time.

"Right Harry get this fucker started. The sooner we get these lifts done the better. Come on Chop, Chop." Pat had made up his mind. Indecision in front of the gang could wreck the team's confidence in him in no time flat. Experience told him it was better to make the wrong choice and be firm about it than skirt around the edges. The men would follow Pats orders through thick and thin. That was part of the unspoken trust that held the team together.

Chapter 18. The Lift.

Within minutes Harry had the big winch engine started again. In the steadily warming late morning, air the engine fired easily. As before Harold ran the engine at half throttle. Carefully watching the temperature gauge. It normally took around five minutes before the white needle began to move behind the once clear glass. Now the build-up of dirt and oil had permanently missed the little glass disc on either side, leaving a relatively clear area in the centre where the little instrument would finally settle down.

Pat dispatched the riggers to ready themselves for coupling up the hook, while a nod from Harold indicated that as far as he could tell there were no problems with the engine. In turn, Harold shut the throttle down to just above low idle nodded to Di Jones.

For the second time that morning the Welshman pulled the long clutch lever back and engaged the gear. A quick look back towards Harold told him the big Scotsman was ready to proceed. Slowly Di pushed the lever forward until he could feel the tension from the thrust bearing.

The rumble from the big eight-cylinder engine deepened as the clutch took up the drive. Producing a single elongated plume of dark fumes from the exhaust. Now the winch drive was running. Both men could feel the low-frequency rumble that told them the big drive rings were now trundling round as normal. This time there were no out of place noises from the equipment. The sound produced by the heavy plant would change as all the mechanical parts warmed up. However, the differences would be almost indistinguishable to all but seasoned operators like Harold and Di.

Pat had moved back from the unfinished pylon to a position halfway between the winch and the gate. Now that the decision had been made, it was back to work as normal. His careful eye roamed over the site, ticking off a mental check-list of all the possible things that might go wrong. First, they should run the ropes back and forward through the blocks to flex and squeeze the water out of the fibres. However, the faint sound made by Thompson's Wellington boots trudging through the muddy top-soil told him that was unlikely to happen.

All the men were now in place. Harold and Rooster stood back behind the tower; ready to ascend when the upper arm had been lifted into position. Tom and Matt Stood inside the outer of the three arms lying on the ground parallel to the pylon base. When he and Di dropped the hook down through the metal frame. They would attach the rope slings to the hook and then get behind the pylon where they would be safe.

If a winch rope broke under tension, the two halves would whip back to one side or another. Anyone caught by the near supersonic velocities achieved by the rope ends would be cut in half. It was generally considered that the safest place to be if that happened was on the opposite side of the pylon, protected by the steel structure.

With a full crew, Pat normally stood about thirty yards beyond the structure in direct line of sight from the control platform of the big winch. There he could direct the lift with little worry about ropes or falling objects. Today Thompson should take up that very same position. Pat had in effect been demoted, now it was he who would have to interpret the less experienced man's signals. The big ganger would have preferred Wing-nut, who at least knew how to signal correctly to take-over his duties as a controller.

Things started well, Thompson at least made his way to the correct spot. Once Pat was satisfied everyone was in position, he himself made his way back to the winch. Taking one last look around before climbing up onto the platform. But! There was one man missing. Thompson had made straight for the climbers. At this distance, Pat had no chance of hearing what was being said over the engine noise. However, it was clear that there was a heated discussion going on. Rooster and Harold were both arguing with the bigger man.

Seconds passed while Pat tarried with the idea of interceding. Then changed his mind. Now that things were rolling it was better to keep them going. No doubt he would get all the gruesome details later.

The argument lasted all of a minute. From Roosters body language Pat could work out with some certainty what punishment the sharp-tongued Scouser would be delivering to the overstuffed and arrogant fool of a civil engineer. Harold had already given up and was marching along the boards toward the leg nearest the lift. Without even looking back the Scotsman threw the clip of his safety harness over his shoulder and began to climb steadily up the leg.

Harold was halfway up the structure before Rooster started climbing. Easily following his partner up towards the landing site almost at the top of the pylon. On reaching the position that the lower part of the arm would be bolted onto the main structure, Harold clipped his safety line onto the cross rope. Then confidently walked across the three-inch wide cross angle to the other side of the pylon. Hooking his line into one of the bolt holes in the vertical support Harold relaxed waiting for Rooster to take up a similar position on the other leg, but this time, above him where the upper angle irons of the arm would connect to the mainframe. Both men made themselves as comfortable as possible.

Neither of the two was in a good temper. Thompson had marched over and ordered them up the pylon. Countermanding one of the most stringent safety rules of the company. The men never went aloft until the arm had been lifted into place. Then and only then would they climb up and land the arm.

during the lift, the two riggers controlled the lift from below. Each had a lighter rope attached to the large end of the load and in conjunction with Pats hand signals, they would keep the heavy object straight until the climbers secured it to the frame. Now, Tom and Matt would have to depend on Thompson's dubious commands to get the lift into the correct position.

From his vantage point near the top of the pylon, Rooster eyed up the new contender for his vengeance spitting out towards Thompson, who stood making a violent handle winding motion in Pat's general direction. The globe of spittle, roughly the size of a seagull shit arched out and away from the pylon, carried on the wind by the slow-moving air.

Rooster smiled as the package landed unseen, just behind the idiot gyrations that were supposed to be legible sign language.

"Just right." He thought unbuttoning his fly and removing his extremely large penis. Balancing easily on the angle he started to pee. Waggling the flaccid member quickly from side to side with his left hand. The result was a shower of rapidly cooling urine falling on and around Mark Thompson. Whether the civil engineer knew it or not, Rooster had his revenge.

distracted by the sudden fall of water droplets, Mark Thompson looked up, confused by the clear sky above. Holding out his hand as if testing for rain as the last few drops landed in the palm of his hand. Rooster had slipped his member back into the safety of his trousers and turned away.

Pat had finally mounted the platform and signalled his readiness to Thompson. He had seen Roosters wicked trick, all the men knew of this foul habit, and most of them had been caught out by it at some time in the past. He smiled as Thompson held out his hand testing for rain. The tosser had an uncanny aim whether it was with a tool, a stone, or his dick. The alcohol laden piss would have the fool smelling of urine all day. Then Pat turned back to the winch controls, taking one last forlorn look back towards the road.

A puff of black smoke drove up from the engine exhaust as pat opened the throttle; bringing the motor up to working revs. Both men could now feel the gentle swaying motion caused by the big brake drums on the winch. A steady swish, swish sound could be heard as the brake bands rubbed the outer surface of the drums free of surface rust. After ten minutes or so the sound would settle down as all the friction surfaces came up near their working temperature.

A nod to Di and the Welshman pulled back the lever engaging the main winch. Slowly the big drum on Di's side began to turn. It would take nearly a full minute to make one revolution. Having a working diameter of five feet, over sixteen feet of rope would be wound on. Di allowed it to turn for only a few seconds, merely taking up the slack on the main lift. Once satisfied that the thick rope was under strain, he shut off the drive to the drum, engaging the holding brake.

They were lifting the outermost of the three arms, laid out parallel to the main frame. First, the arm would have to be lifted vertically. Using both winches together in the manner of a death slide, it was normal to first lift the arm up allowing it to clear the other two. Then co-coordinating both winches, move the airborne object in towards the tower. The two lighter ropes allowed the two riggers to steer the thick end round so that it then pointed towards the main structure.

Chapter 19. The Block.

"So far so good." Thought Pat as the first arm hovered about five feet above the ground, the weight of the arm pulling inwards tensioning the control rope. Now it was Pats turn to engage his winch, pulling the load back, outwards and up away from the other two arms. The rope Jumped, creating a twang that vibrated right around the full rig. Slamming the Brake on and disengaging the drive, Pat Swore. There could only be one reason for the control rope snapping tight like that. The block on the anchor must have seized. Making the rope jump around the outer surface of the pulley.

This was the reason the winch-man always worked their rig before attempting a lift. Now they were really fucked. The only other block that could handle this type of load had been damaged and was unserviceable.

"God knows what idiot idea Thompson would come up with now." Thought Pat as he took a quick look up at the climbers. What he saw told him they were not liking this at all. On the odd occasions where it had been necessary to send them up top like today, everything had always gone perfectly. The violent twang had sent shock-waves right around the pylon structure. Causing both men to hang on tight. This was not a good start to the operation.

Pat held both arms straight up in the air, waiting till all the men had stopped and were looking towards him. When he was satisfied he had all their attention, still holding his right arm extended, pointed his index finger downwards making a circular motion with the extended digit.

All the men with the exception of Mark Thompson instantly knew that the lift was about to be lowered back to the ground. When each had acknowledged using a variety of different signals, Pat lowered his arm and nodded to Di Jones.

Seconds later the arm again rested on the same pile of railway sleepers it had been on just a few moments before. Di stopped as the main lift rope began to slacken. Pat continued making the downward twirling motion, indicating that he wanted the line extended until the rig went slack. Another dangerous move. If the rope wound slack and the drum continued to rotate, then the rope still on the drum could slacken off and tangle.

Next, the riggers would have to disconnect the hook from the slings. If there wasn't enough slack, then they probably would have to try and pull some off the drum, a yard or two at a time.

Thompson was incensed; he couldn't understand why Pat had stopped the lift. He had no comprehension of what the loud thwack had implied. As far as he was concerned the big Irishman was at it again. Bellowing and gesticulating violently till his cheeks were bright red. Thompson tried to make Pat restart the lift. However, the Irishman was totally ignoring him.

Tom looked for Pat's signal to disconnect. As soon as the main drum stopped Pat waved Tom on. A second motion with his hand sent Matt out towards the anchor now that is was safe to walk along the ground ropes. Pat pulled the strangler on the big winch engine. Then jumped down and made for the other County. Followed by Di Jones who had first secured the winch before following his boss.

Things didn't look good, Two feet from the block a section of the rope nearly a foot long looked swollen and black. This was what happened when ropes were left wet too long. The black area had been rusted and frozen to the rim of the pulley. Which in turn had seized to the block casing. The bush in the centre had obviously broken up on one side and locked the wheel solid. Now, what were they going to do?

Pat barely had a chance to inspect the frozen pulley when Mark Thompson arrived and began shouting at him for stopping the lift.

"What the fucks wrong now?" Snapped Thompson. Still not comprehending the seriousness of the situation. Frankly, he didn't care.

"Can't you see the pulley is fucked?" Snapped Pat. His patience was wearing very thin.

"Well fix it, man." Mark Thompson bellowed back.

"We can't. Mike was going to have a look at it before he left, but after your tantrums, he had to go. He won't have another until the end of next week." Pat had now given up any intention of showing this fool respect. Now it was personal.

"So why don't you just fuck off and let us get on with our jobs." Pat was several inches shorter than Mark Thompson. However, he held his ground, looking defiantly into the angry engineer's face.

"How dare you talk to me like that you ignorant Irish moron. I'll see you fired for this. Now fix the fucking thing and let's get on with this shambles.

"And how do you suggest we fix it?" Growled Pat. Now as visibly angry as his adversary.

"Do you have a spare?"

"Yes, but it's damaged."

"Is it free."

"Yes. But the securing ring is bent. We can't get a shackle through it."

"Can't you tie it to the post."

"It wouldn't be safe. If it failed, we could lose the pylon." Pat could have kicked himself. He knew the instant he uttered the words that he had just given the fool engineer his chance. Now they would really be in the shit.

"I'm not taking the responsibility if you lash that pulley to the anchor."

"Nobody's asking you to. Now get the fucking block over here." Thompson sneered at Pat.

The big Irishman swithered for a moment. Every bone in his body wished to deck this arrogant fool there and then. Then he thought better of it. If the pylon ended up fucked, he would make damn sure Thompson would carry the blame.

Still holding Thompson's glare, Pat instructed Tom to get the other block and the tools. Having been split once already this morning it would only take a few minutes to disconnect the two halves. The block could then be slipped over the rope. It should then take minutes to re-connect the two sides.

Tom returned to find Pat and Thompson doing their best to ignore each other.

"What you want us to do with this Pat?"

"Ask this fool. He seems to know better than all of us." Now the lines had been drawn Pat had no intention of letting Thompson feel anything other than unwanted. Pats now obvious frontal attack had shown Mark Thompson that it was possible he had underestimated the big ganger. Common-sense should have told him you don't get the type of result this man did if you were a moron.

Perhaps it had been a mistake to think that he could get more from the top squad in the company. The thought barely had time to form before his arrogance took over and dismissed it completely. He was the educated man here and they jolly well better get used to it. After all, Oxford was one of the top universities in the country. How dare this man think he was an equal.

Now as the damaged block was thrown down at his feet, Thompson began to see what Pat had been talking about. It was obvious even to him that there was no way a shackle pin could pass through the damaged securing ring.

"Can't you take the insides from this one and put them in that one?" Asked Thompson, barely managing to hide the doubt in his voice.

This time it was Tom who dived in,

"The bushes in this one have been modified. There's no way you can do that." Thompson visibly chewed over his next question, but Tom got in first.

"And No, you can't straighten the ring. The metal has been stretched out of shape. If you try to straighten it. Most likely it would break." Now Mark Thompson was cornered. Here was another apparent moron questioning his authority. Oh, not directly, but this time using science and common-sense. Again, the little voice of doubt was tramped down.

"You're a rigger, lash it to the post." Snapped the big civil engineer, visibly daring Tom to challenge him once again.

Now Tom was caught in the same trap Pat had been. If he failed to obey the direct order he might be sacked. However, the idea did have its merits. Tom had to do exactly that many times in Africa and India. Unlike Matt, he did know exactly how to safely lash the block to the post.

Tom looked at Pat for confirmation. Pat knew that Tom could do exactly what the fool suggested. In a way, he was happier now that it had been resolved. The big

Irishman nodded. All the men knew Tom wouldn't do anything that would jeopardise their safety. Again, the men set to their work. The decision had been made and it was up to them to carry out the order.

From his vantage point high up on the pylon Harold had a fair idea of what had happened. Tom had been right about the block. The sudden frost had altered the metal structure just enough for it to fail under load. The ageing and sometimes quite sullen rigger shared the same uncanny ability he himself had to somehow sense when mechanical equipment was about to fail.

Harold felt sorry for Pat left to fend off the arrogant ministries of that fool Thompson. He and idiots like him were the main reason Harold had refused a gaffer's job. He'd seen the same sort of stupidity in the army. Men promoted into positions they were not suited for. It never worked out. But in the end, there was always a result. Not from the direct order but from the blood sweat and tears of the ordinary buck private who had to try and make the nonsensical order work.

After a few minutes, Gerry made his way to the truck. Returning with a new coil of three-quarter rope. That could only mean one thing. Tom was going to lash the block to the post. Good! At least it would be done properly. The rigger had an uncanny way of securing things with rope. Harold remembered asking Tom about where he had learned this skill.

Tom had been in the Navy as a young man, stationed as a seaman on one of His Majesties few remaining sailing ships. Ropes and brute strength had been a way of life for him as a teenager. Later when he had left the navy and joined an international construction company. the skills learned as a seaman had saved his skin from seashore to steaming jungle. Harold knew the block wouldn't fail once Tom had lashed it to the anchor post.

A glance over and up told him Rooster was sleeping. The idiot just hunkered down with his back to the vertical support, rested his head on his knees and went to sleep. All that would stop him from falling was his safety line clipped on a foot above his head. Harold remembered the first time he had seen Rooster do this. Pat had ripped him from arse to elbow, more because of how he felt himself than any fear of the lad falling to his death. Now all knew better than disturb the fool until they were ready to start again.

Chapter 20. Timeout.

Harold made himself comfortable. There wasn't any point going back down. Tom and Matt would have the pulley changed in around ten minutes. Time for a fag. Leaning up against the inside of the vertical support, his feet planted on the two horizontal angles. Harold had no problem rolling a cigarette.

Taking a deep pull his thoughts turned back to Mavis and the expected child. This was one day he would remember for the rest of his life. The thought of Mavis developing a substantial lump was surprisingly pleasing even erotic. It would be interesting to feel the baby kicking. Perhaps he would even be able to listen to the baby's heart. Would the bump be hard or soft and squishy like her shapely breasts? How would it feel to run his fingertips over the bulge?

This was a new experience for Harold. The men seldom talked about the mechanics of childbearing. That was left to the wives. Nevertheless, Harold decided that he wanted to be a part of the process. How would it affect Mavis, what would be the first signs?

Morning sickness should be the first. So far Mavis hadn't had that problem. What else? Cravings. Yes, at some point there would be cravings. Mave has some strange tastes as it was. Pineapple chunks and pickled onions. The thought of it turned his mouth sour for a second.

He would have to build a crib for the child. Later on, he would be able to make wooden toys, possibly a little trolley filled with coloured wooden blocks. He could build wooden jigsaws or carve little animals. A toy farmyard for a boy or a wooden dolls house if it was a girl.

In two or three years they may even have to get a bigger van. That would bring problems of its own. The current one could be towed on the road with no problem. A larger one would have to be moved on the back of a lorry. Still, they would have plenty of time to worry about things like that.

Maybe tonight they should walk up to the phone box and call his mum. She would be pleased, several times over the past four years she had suggested it was time they started a family. Not directly, a little hint here, a nudge there. The old girl never said much, but when she did, you usually got it directly between the eyes. He supposed it was a consequence of living with the old man for so many years.

Harold had no doubt the old bugger would be glad Mave was pregnant. However, it was more likely he would try and use it to get them to come home. That was not such a happy thought. Really there were only two options now, either take on the gaffer's job or give up this life and go home. Slowly he scanned the surrounding countryside. Whatever happened he wouldn't be doing much more of this.

This was one of the most satisfying parts of the job. The view from each pylon was unique. Even from day to day, creating a constantly changing panorama, exquisitely coloured by changing wind and weather. On the ground, the air could be still, yet up here near the top of the spindly structure the wind could be cutting along at a fair pace. The chilling cold could be a major problem. It was just as well Mave had given him the new long-john's. They were a bit itchy at the moment but after a few washes, the cotton material would soften a bit, making them even warmer.

Off in the distance, he could just make out Mike O'mahony's van parked at the red phone box. That was good if he returned they might get the two winches serviced after all. No doubt there would be another confrontation between Mike and the idiot Thompson.

Mike could be a bastard in his own way when circumstances required it. However, one thing the ageing mechanic was well known for was his fairness and generally good nature. He naturally inspired men to work for him. They may grumble but in general, his fitters would follow him to the ends of the earth and back. He was a bit like Pat in many ways. Both men had a similar effect on the men in their charge.

If he could inspire similar feelings in his own men then he could build a top-notch squad around himself. But who would he end up with? Mike Simpson wouldn't give him numb-skulls to start with. Perhaps some of the men from this squad might come with him. Matt and Di Jones were both due for a promotion. He knew and trusted both. Gerry would be another good choice.

One person, he didn't want was Rooster. Even he recognised the young man's skills as a climber. However, the minute his feet touched the ground it was like another man jumped into his boots. Pat often swore the only reason he kept him around was for entertainment value. His antics were usually cruelly comical. A wry smile formed on his lips, in a way he would miss the idiot. Still, it was possible he would collect one of his own over the coming years.

His thoughts drifted back to Mavis and the morning they had literally fallen for each other. Mave's parents had been killed in a fire when she was only two. Leaving the young girl to be brought up by an aunt and uncle. Arthur her uncle was spot on, her aunt was a bitch. The old cow had been unable to have children of her own. Taking Mave on had seemed to be an ideal substitute. However, the reality was completely different. Kate was a viciously jealous woman. She hated the fact that her sister had children and she couldn't. Even now Mave still bore the brunt of her adopted mother's wrath. Arthur, on the other hand, doted on his niece. Which probably made his wicked wife hate Mave even more. There was no accounting for families.

Arthur would be over the moon if he ever got the word. Mave wrote to him regularly but going by the infrequent replies, the letters were being intercepted. Harold smiled, he could see Arthur in one of the huge greenhouses at Mauldslie estate near Rosebank on Clydeside where he was employed as head gardener. One thing was certain, Arthur would spoil the child rotten.

More voices drifted up from below. Pat and the engineer were at it again. Gerry was running over from the store with a roped set of tackle. Basically, two pulley blocks and a length of rope. By the sound of it Thompson was shouting again. This time it seemed to be Tom who was on the receiving end of the bastard's wrath.

An occasional cloud low down and far to the south drifted in front of the sun. Bringing a chill as they passed into shadow. A distant blast from a ship's horn, sounded as it steadily made its way up the canal towards Manchester. Even further away from the large cooling towers of Inch, A power station set a steady stream of steam up into the cold clear atmosphere. The site they lived on lay less than a mile from the station. His thoughts turned back to Mavis. was she at home or had she taken the train into town. He would find out later.

His attention turned to a flock of crows that had risen noisily from the small wood about half a mile away. Their aggravated calls echoing clearly over the open space. They circled excitedly for some moments before either landing back in the trees or scattering in different directions.

The noise from the angry crows woke Rooster. At first glance, he looked disorientated, yet his balance remained rock solid. After a huge rift, followed by a loud fart, he reached into his open donkey jacket and retrieved a pouch of tobacco. Without care or concern, he quickly rolled a fag. Lighting it with a battered petrol lighter.

"What's happening Harry?" he asked almost pleasantly.

"They're changing the block on the anchor. Looks like Tom is going to lash the one you buggered to the post."

"Will it hold?" said Rooster lazily after taking another drag at his fag.

"Should be all right. Tom knows what he's doing."

"Any sign of that baldy old bastard O'mahony?" asked Rooster changing the subject.

"His van's still sitting at the phone box." Answered Harold.

Rooster giggled.

"That should be fun when he comes back. That stupid fucker will find his dick flapping in the wind. Serves him right." It was obvious that Rooster found such confrontations amusing.

Chapter 21. The phone call.

For the most part, Mike O'mahony had little trouble with the civil engineering staff. However, like all organisations, there is always one man who stands out above the rest. Thompson defiantly held that position. At fifty he had been passed over for every major promotion in the last five years. Now it seemed he had decided to take a different tack. If he could woo Nena Blenkinsopp, then Mike had no doubt he would use this to his advantage. What the fool didn't know was there had been subtle moves inside the board to remove her brother from his precarious position as managing director.

Mike smiled. It would be ironic if Thompson married Nena Blenkinsopp only to find her and her brother out of a job. Oh, that would be poetic justice. He had never liked the arrogant fool. The bastard would roar into the workshop, jump out and order the nearest mechanic to fix his Landrover. Giving little heed to proper procedure. Every time he came to the workshop Mike ended up in a heated argument with him.

This morning had been an exception. Mike had just had enough of the fool. It was time someone clipped his wings and the engineering manager had proven himself fit for him. Unfortunately, due to his pillow connections, it was prudent to make sure of the ground he stood on.

It was better to keep Mike Simpson abreast of the situation and guarantee his colleagues support than to have it all fall to pieces next week. Thompson would be gambling on him not being able to find the regional manager easily. Fortunately, Mike O'mahony knew exactly where his friend would be, and more importantly when he would be there.

For the first time in over six months, Mike Simpson had decided to take some time off. He and his wife Merrill would be travelling down to Somerset to spend a week on her brother's farm. They had been talking about it the previous day, after the discussions about Harold and the new gang.

Mike smiled as he thought about Merrill. She was one of those women who just got on with things. Born and brought up on the farm she knew what it was to work hard. Any time he had visited their home, she had always been found in her massive garden, dressed in jeans and an old shirt. Pushing a barrow filled with gathered weeds or discarded plants.

Another of Merrill's talents was her ability to take the most basic ingredients and turn them into a fabulous meal fit for kings. Summer and winter there was always a big pot of vegetable soup boiling on the Aga. Visitors could always look forward to a big plate of the delicious steaming liquid accompanied by huge lumps of fresh home-baked bread. Mikes mouth watered at the thought of it if only his own wife could cook like that woman.

Mike found the phone box without any problem. Pulling the van up onto the verge. He jumped out and made his way into the red phone box. Unlike the ones in town, this one was spotlessly clean. It was obvious that the ladies in the local community took turns to clean and polish this box regularly. A small cloth bag filled with dried lavender had been hung over the big black metal phone. Even the two silver buttons marked A and B had been polished to a high sheen. Being an opportunist Mike habitually pressed the B button first, just to make sure the previous occupant hadn't been able to get their call connected and left without their change. No such luck today.

Mike lifted the heavy Bakelite hand-piece and dialled 100, listening to the rhythmic clicks as the dial slowly moved back to the rest position. Listening to the pulsed sound a stray thought entered Mikes mind. Someday they would invent a phone with buttons instead of the rotary dial.

Then the operator answered, killing the stray thought forever. Mike asked to be connected to the number in Somerset. Then while the operator waited for the connection to be made, informed him of how much to place in the rounded hump that held the penny slot.

It took nearly a minute for the call to be connected. Then the operator cleared the line and left him listening to the repetitive ringtones. Like most rural houses it sometimes took a while for the homeowners to make it to the phone. Mikes In-Laws were fairly well off and employed a housekeeper. Luckily that meant there was always someone in the house.

Finally, the housekeeper answered the phone. She had a thick Somerset accent that just sounded warm and pleasant.

"Good morning this is Maple Farm. How may I help you?" Mike had met her once, Mrs Brown, a widow in her late sixties. She was a little plump woman with round glasses, a flowery apron which almost always seemed to be covered in white flower. Her husband had been a farm worker and unfortunately, he had been killed in an accident with a binder, some years before. Merrill's family had offered her the job as house-keeper shortly afterwards. The tied house she and her husband had lived in had to be vacated for the new workers family. Now the old girl had a room of her own above the kitchen.

He could imagine her standing in the hall under the polished wooden bannister rail. Trying to keep the flower from her apron from dusting up the spotless hall furniture.

Mike pressed button A and answered,

"Hello, Mrs Brown. This is Mike O'mahony."

"Oh, Mr O'mahony I remember you. It's some time since we saw you down here. How can I help you?" Mike loved her thick musical accent. If left alone he could listen to her talking all day.

"I'd like to leave a message for Mike Simpson. He and Merrill are on their way down at the moment. Can you ask Mike to call me at this number as soon as possible when he arrives?"

"Certainly, Mr O'mahony. I have a pencil here. What is the number?" Mike read the number from the engraved plate on the front of the metal phone box.

"Is there a message I can pass on sir?"

"No. Please ask him to call me as soon as possible. I'm in Cheshire. He will know what it's about."

Mike exchanged a few pleasantries with Mrs Brown and then politely finished the call. It was only ten thirty-five. The Simpson's weren't due to arrive until at least eleven. Mike would have to content himself till the phone rang.

The thought of Merrill Simpson's soup made him hungry. Thompson had interrupted breakfast, chasing all thoughts of food from his mind. Now in the peace and quiet of this little back road, he could sit and finish his tea.

Mike contented himself taking time out to enjoy the warming sunshine. Mike Simpson had told him to call after he had spoken with Harold about the gaffers job. So far, he hadn't managed to get a word with the mild-mannered Scotsman. Thompson's intervention had disrupted all his plans. One thing was certain once he had spoken with Mike Simpson, whatever the verdict, he would have to return to the site. He found the thought of having to maul Thompson again that morning distasteful. Hopefully the arrogant fool had stayed away.

Over the years Mike had seen many Thompson's come and go. Unfortunately, they were not in the minority. It appeared to be part of the qualification. It was worrying to think that someone could spend four or five years at a university like Oxford or Cambridge, qualify without ever being on a site then be given the keys to a company where men's lives were at risk. At best it would be another four or five years rubbing shoulders with men like Pat before most of them really began to understand the true nature of what they had trained for.

Some of them were bright kids. One, in particular, the first woman Civil engineer to be employed by the company. Anna had been her name. Had been one smart cookie. She could wrap most of the site managers around her little finger. However, unlike Thompson, she listened to every word the foremen said before making an assessment of the situation. In most cases, the problem was resolved quickly and efficiently.

He chuckled to himself. She was an extremely attractive brunette, with a figure any actress would covet. Unfortunately, after five years or so she married a pillock much like Thompson, and left a year later to have a baby. She visited them from time to time, but it was obvious her husband and his family were doing a number on her. They seemed to be turning her into the stereotypical dutiful wife, trapped at home with the dogs and the children. It was a crying shame. She had been a bloody good engineer.

At five past eleven, the phone rang, shocking Mike from his reverie. It only took him seconds to rush back to the box and lift the receiver.

"Mike O'mahony here. Is that you Mike?"

"Yes. Has Harold accepted the job?"

"Sorry, Mike I haven't had a chance to talk to him yet. There's another more delicate situation developing here. I need your counsel on this one." Mike Simpson knew there must be a real problem. his colleague had only slightly less standing in the company than himself. for Mike O'mahony to ask for his advice meant that there really was something potentially devastating afoot.

Mike Simpson listened intently to Mike's rendition of Thompson's behaviour. Now it became clear that his association with Nena Blenkinsopp had seriously compromised the managing director's position. Not that that was a bad thing. Nigel Blenkinsopp was a fool. This was just the very situation his opponents had been waiting for.

The challenger was well known to Mike Simpson. He was twenty years younger and at his best. The younger man would be a much-needed breath of fresh air, just when the company needed it most.

When the background situation was revealed to Mike O'mahony it was clear to both men that the company would most likely have a new managing director and one less civil engineer by the middle of next week. It was a relief for both men that such a potentially damaging dynasty was about to fall. Blenkinsopp and his cronies were remnants of a time and empire now falling apart at the seams and dying from the rot within.

Chapter 22. Once again.

Pat dragged his large watch from the depths of his pocket. Ten past eleven. Tom and Matt had made a beautiful job of lashing the block to the anchor post. The big foreman was so confident he would bet his own life that it wouldn't fail. Tom had woven a figure of eight around both the block and the post. Interlacing each turn of the thinner rope in such a manner as to avoid depending on the bent shackle ring. In fact, the eye was now superfluous having only three turns of the rope passing through it, there only to stop the block from slipping rather than for any means of support.

Although he wouldn't admit it, Thompson was pleased with the result. Maybe these men weren't such a shower of morons. He might even be able to do something with them after all.

"Right, now that you have finished playing with your toys. Can we get this show on the road?" Growled Thompson to the knot of men around the busted block. Gerry who was undoing the last of the bolts holding the two halves of the seized block together received a nudge with the engineer's boot.

Matt saw the nudge and angrily turned on Thompson.

"No. This rope is sodden and may well be rotting from the core. If we go ahead and this fails it will be on your head."

"The ropes only damp you fool. Now let's get this show on the road." Matt looked angrily towards Pat. The big Irishman merely nodded, indicating that the men should follow Thompson's orders. Pat didn't like it either, but they had worked with ropes far worse than this. With careful handling, the tension created by the lift would quickly drive the moisture from the twisted fibres. On a day like this, it would only be a matter of hours before the rope dried out.

Gerry picked up the two halves of the busted pulley block. Tom had been correct, one bush had broken up and jammed digging into both the shaft and the wheel, stopping it cold. Even if the pin and bushes in the other block had been the same size, due to the damage caused by the broken bush. It was doubtful if they would have been able to fit the replacement parts.

From his vantage point, Harold watched the men move back towards their stations.

"Right Rooster looks like we're ready to roll."

"Thank fuck for that my arse is going to sleep." Replied the Scouser, pulling himself erect, while rubbing his numb bum with his free hand.

By the time Pat reached the winch engine Both Harold and Rooster had re-positioned themselves ready to land the arm. The big Irishman waited until all the men were in their correct positions and had signalled their readiness before starting the big eight-cylinder engine. Even Thompson Had raised his right arm and held it aloft until each of the others had visibly acknowledged their readiness in a similar manner.

Pat looked up, waiting for the signal from Harold that indicated readiness. A nod from Rooster and Harold waved, then held his free hand high above his head. They were ready.

Pat turned the key, the big engine turned over slowly. The batteries were getting past their best. Normally the engine would run all day, bringing the charge level back up to maximum, ready for the next day. However, the extended effort due to the cold, then having the engine shut down twice without having a chance to build up much charge, had severely depleted their capacity.

Wow, Wow, then the engine fired. Pat heaved a sigh of relief. If the big motor had failed to start. It would have taken another half hour, to replace the battery with one from either the truck of the other county. Pat let the engine run at half throttle for a minute before pulling the throttle back to idle. Once again, He checked the men.

All was in order, he nodded to Di. Again, the big clutch lever was hauled back and the drive engaged. The rhythmic swaying causing both operators to instinctively compensate for the motion. Unconsciously changing their balance as the platform moved gently back and forth.

Tom gave the signal that he and Matt were ready. Thompson raised his right arm, indicating he was ready. Pat answered their signals and opened the throttle again bringing the engine up to working speed.

A nod from both riggers and Pat gave Mark Thompson the thumbs up. The ganger pointed to his eyes and then towards the engineer. Signalling to all the men that he had handed control over. Now they would find out what kind of metal the civil engineer was made of.

Now that the lift was finally under-way Thompson had calmed down. during the makeshift repairs to the block, he had begun to reform his opinions of the squad. It was ironic that they as a team were actually doing to him what he had set about doing to them. It was like two rival males posturing over their territory. Thompson was the usurper trying to take control of Pats extended family. They had faced up to each other and after a fairly vicious battle, Pat and the men had acceded to his authority. However, during the battle, he had been forced to modify his own behaviour, just enough for the foreman and his squad to grudgingly accept him. Pats careful checking before handing over control was as much an effort to help him succeed as it was a last chance to ensure the safety of the men under his charge.

Thompson suddenly felt very lonely. All the men had their eyes on him. Only one man seemed to have nothing to do. The lad they called Wing-nut stood by the mobile store. Apparently, he had nothing to do during the lift.

Thompson swallowed, two sets of eyes would be better than one. Copying the "Come Here" he had seen Pat use earlier on. The engineer pointed at Gerry then patted his forehead. Instantly without hesitation, the lanky lad started towards him. No-one else moved. The rest of the men stood patiently waiting for his next command.

"Stand behind me lad. Tap me on the shoulder if I miss anything." Gerry raised his eyebrows. He had been expecting another bollocking.

"Yes, sir." Replied the boy taking up position beside Thompson. Just as he would when Pat controlled the lift. The ganger normally had his attention on the position of the arm, depending on Gerry informing him of any problem developing on the ground.

"Sir."

"Yes."

"Pat normally keeps his eyes on the lift. He gets me to tell him what's happening on the ground." Mark Thompson marvelled. Even the boy was trying to give him the benefit of the doubt.

"Ok, you just do the same for me." He replied uncharacteristically in a mild but firm voice.

One last look towards each man then,

"Ready Lad?"

"Yes, sir." Then raising his right hand straight up into the air he began opening and closing motion with his hand. Signalling that Di Jones should inch the lift upwards allowing the rig to take up the strain.

Slowly the lift rope inched upward until the slings connected to the arm pulled tight. Mark Thompson Showed the flat of his hand to the winch-men, holding it there until he received a nod from both riggers.

A look up the tower received the thumbs up from Rooster indicating that both climbers were ready.

"Okay lad."

"All clear Mr Thompson." Replied Gerry.

Chapter 23. Oh Shit!

Pat smiled. Good! Gerry would be exactly where he could do the most good. Thompson was an experienced engineer who should know how to control a lift. If he hadn't done it himself then he would have witnessed it numerous time over the years. Allowing Gerry to assist him at least showed he did have some semblance of sense.

On command, Di engaged the winch and released the brake. Allowing the big drum to rotate winding on the thick rope. Then came the command to halt. Thompson had seen the tension increasing in the ground portion of the control rope. The arm was now hovering some six inches above the now-vacant railway sleepers. Rotating slowly clockwise against a steady pressure from Matt's control rope.

Matt looked for confirmation from Thompson. The engineer nodded, indicating that Matt had control until the arm had reached the correct orientation with the thick end pointing towards the tower.

Normally, under Pat's control, this would be done while the lift was in progress. However, Mark Thompson's inexperience stopped him from trying anything fancy.

As the arm reached the correct orientation, Tom brought pressure to bear on his side of the arm. Stopping the rotation and holding the arm in place, ready to be lifted.

Again, all eyes turned to Thompson.

"Ok lad?"

"Okay sir, everyone's ready." Again, he visually checked all the men then began to rotate his up-stretched finger in a clockwise direction.

Di Jones released the brake and the drum began to turn again. Allowing the arm to move slowly upward. Both Tom and Matt had begun to walk away from the arm, paying out their control ropes while still keeping enough tension to hold the arm in position.

Pat waited as the arm rose almost vertically upwards. Until pressure from the control rope began to pull the lift away from the tower.

Pat watched Thompson. Gerry leaned forward towards the man and the halt signal was given. Di stopped the lift. The arm now hung in the air approximately thirty feet up. Still not high enough to clear the other two arms.

Thompson extended his arm pointing towards the tower. Pat disengaged the drive and tentatively released the brake. Slowly under expert control, the arm began to arc downwards towards the tower.

As the arm approached its sibling, still laid out on the ground. Thompson moved his arm directly above his head holding the flat of his hand towards Pat. The ganger applied the brake and the arm stopped, swaying gently under the pressure from the two riggers. The signal changed, and Di again started to lift.

The process was repeated four times until the arm hung just a few feet from the tower about a quarter of the way up the structure. Thompson was in no hurry now.

Pat was surprised, even a little impressed. The man's signals were clear and concise. He was making up for the lack of experience with ladles of caution. The upward procession was slow and precise, leaving little room for mistake.

Up and then in. Ten or so feet at a time. This had been the very method he himself had used at first. It wasn't fast, but it was safe. On the fourth inward movement of the load, Pat felt the brake lever mushy. There was more slack in its travel than before. However, the brake still engaged.

Now the top two angles were just a few feet below Harold. Suddenly the brake lever in Pat's hand went slack. Inside the console, a clevis pin connecting the long control rod to the brake actuator had come loose. Mark Thompson's earlier attempts to fit the PTO shaft had dislodged a worn split pin. The very same object that had so effectively ripped open the arm of his suit jacket. This shouldn't have been a problem. The brake should come on automatically stopping the winch from winding out.

Di had just engaged the main winch to lift the load another ten feet or so when a loud bang locked the winch lever in gear. The now loose brake control rod had swung backwards and down, catching on the yoke of the power take-off shaft.

The clevis bent and jammed against the rotating shaft, caught in this manner it was forced back upwards at high speed. The lever flew from Pat's hand, nearly breaking his powerful fingers. The force of the strike jamming the now severely distorted control rod out of shape locking it against the clutch and brake lever for the main winch.

Realising what had happened Di Jones frantically pulled at the control lever to disengage the drive. Pat was out of it. His hand was almost useless from the impact. Di couldn't even kill the engine as the only working strangler was on Pats side of the console. Disengaging the main clutch would mean dropping the arm nearly the height of the tower hitting the structure, possibly throwing the two climbers to their deaths.

Just as the main lift and control lines reached their maximum tension. Di managed to jump over the control console and pull the strangler, killing the big diesel engine. Pat was holding his injured hand close to his body, fighting the pain, struggling to get to his feet.

Even to Mark Thompson, it was obvious there was a problem with the winch. Without question, the engineer held both hands high in a signal for everyone to stop.

Both Tom and Matt had been dragged along with the ascending arm, barely managing to hold on. Now the lift swung gently some twenty feet out from the tower. Stabilised by the ropes held by the two riggers.

Up top, both climbers saw the arm swing away from the tower. Out far enough that they could feel the structure bending with the sudden extra strain.

"Fuck this Harry!" Shouted Rooster, clipping his safety line onto the guide rope and retreating nimbly along the three-inch wide angle to the far side of the structure away from any danger.

The structure settled groaning from the stress applied by the control rope. Harold Hung on. The arm was well above him, even if it swung in it should miss him. As long as they didn't panic things would be ok.

Mike O'mahony turned back to the van after finishing his call with Mike Simpson. A glance in the direction of the site outlined two men high up on the pylon structure. Even at this distance, the black masses of the men were easily discernible.

Mike O'mahony swore violently. This could only mean one thing. Thompson had come back and forced the squad into going ahead with the lift.

The chief mechanic angrily fired up the van and did a hasty three-point turn, managing to break one of the bulbous orange indicator glasses on the driver's side at the rear. Jamming the gear stick into first he accelerated back down the lane towards the erection site. As the gaps in the high hedges flashed past at high-speed Mike could see the arm slowly making its way upwards.

The little van flew past a farmhouse scattering a number of chickens that had been scratching for food on the grass verge. Mike didn't even notice them. By the time the little Morris van screamed to a halt in front of the four tonner. The winch had failed, and the load had been pulled out from the pylon.

Mike ran to the gate just in time to see the control rope break halfway between the load and the anchor. In slow motion, the arm began to arch in towards the pylon. Accelerating steadily as the pendulum effect converted the force of gravity into horizontal motion. Even at that distance, it was obvious that one of the climbers was in trouble.

Harold heard the sound made by the damp fibres snapping inside the control rope. He turned looking out towards the hanging arm, even now beginning to accelerate down towards him. Time slowed, bringing a detached clarity to Harold's mind. He knew instantly what was about to happen but remained calm. Behind him, he could hear Rooster screaming for him to move out of the way. But there was nowhere to go. His safety harness was hooked through a hole in the heavy upright. Unlike the rope, it didn't allow him much lateral movement. All he could expect to do was try and retreat behind the big vertical support and hold on.

"Move Harry! Get the fuck out of there!" Screamed Rooster. Helpless to do anything for his climbing mate.

Pat heard the unmistakable sound of the rope snapping under strain just as the winch engine fell silent. Suddenly the pain in his hand dissipated as it became apparent that his friend was in trouble.

Di Jones swallowed hard, caught between the seconds as the arm accelerated towards Harold and the pylon. Shock and total disbelief fought to numb his mind. Insulating him from the horrific reality of the incident.

Mike O'mahony didn't even feel the cold water as his left leg went down into the water-filled rut catapulting him forward into the same hole Mike Thompson had landed in earlier that day. He lay there clenching a handful of wet soil in each hand as the arm struck the pylon body.

Harold barely moved as the upper angle of the arm smashed the clip of his harness as it just scuffed by the upright.

"This is going to hurt." He thought as the end of the angle iron contacted the left side of his stomach, throwing him backwards free from the structure.

Rooster watched stunned as Harold's form accelerated backwards pushed by the corner angle of the arm. Half a second later the arm grounded out against the main pylon frame violently shaking the whole structure, almost dislodging the shocked scouser from his place of relative safety at the opposite side of the pylon.

Mark Thompson stared in disbelief as the climber's body banged its way down through the cross pieces on the inside of the tower. The body fell silently, stopping briefly only when it hit the structure. No sound passed from the engineer's pale lips.

Standing beside him, Gerry only uttered one word. Harold's name. Then the boy fell silent in shock and disbelief.

Tom and Matt were unaware of what was happening above. As soon as the rope broke both dropped the control ropes and ran for cover. If the arm broke free and fell, they were closest to the pylon, and therefore in imminent danger of being clobbered by the falling framework.

Harold relaxed. There was no point in trying to struggle. Nothing he could do would make any difference to the outcome. Something in his brain took over as the shock switched off and pain signals. The angle iron had buried its self on the left-hand side of his stomach. He had felt the soft structures below the skin tearing from sudden impact. Then he was falling through space, the inside of the pylon retreating from him as he fell towards the ground.

Something hit him in the back causing a horrific snapping sound as his spine parted in two at the point of impact. Still, there was no pain as he tumbled face down towards the ground. A lower cross brace caught him on the calves breaking both legs below the knees, flipping him over once again.

He knew he was falling. Then he was stopped, staring up through the metal structure still ringing from the impact, at the bright blue sky. There had been no transition, his shocked mind had cancelled out the impact.

Harold's vision began to grey out around the edges converting the blue sky into a corridor of bright light. Nothing mattered any-more. Not the sound of Rooster screaming his name high above. Not Pat shouting as he raced to his dying friend's side. Only one thought mattered as a silent word formed on his lips as the tunnel of light closed in around him and life drained from his battered and broken body.

"Mavis."

The end.

Authors Note

The events depicted in this novel are fictional created form several events that have happen around me during my life. Including the death of my father in an accident similar to the one described here. Some of the characters may resemble people that I have worked with during my life. If you are one of them then take the depiction as a sign of respect for you and all the people I have worked with.

This is from a working man to working men, wherever they are.
RM Smart
(And yes there was a character exactly like Rooster.)

Printed in Dunstable, United Kingdom

67460862R00058